Pasqualino Acquaviva

and

Giambone

Frank A. Merola

DEDICATION

To the memory of my Father's dear friend
Giuseppe Di Lucca – "Jumbo" -- "Giambone".
Requiescat in Pace

CONTENTS

Acknowledgments   *i*

Chapter 1   1

Chapter 2   7

Chapter 3   19

Chapter 4   29

Chapter 5   31

Chapter 6   37

Chapter 7   41

Chapter 8   49

Chapter 9   59

Chapter 10   83

Chapter 11   103

Chapter 12   113

Chapter 13   125

Chapter 14   145

Chapter 15   157

Chapter 16   163

Chapter 17   191

Chapter 18   203

Chapter 19   219

Final Chapter   227

Images   249

ACKNOWLEDGMENTS

To the people of Monteforte Cilento, Provincia di Salerno, Italia

For doing the hard, painstaking work of reading through and editing this book, I want to express my love and thanks to my dear wife, Bea.

Thanks, too, to my Zio Luigi, my Zia Veneranda, Mom, Nunzio, The Bernardsville Public Library, and to the memory of my Father, Giuseppe Merola, and his hermit-friend Giuseppe di Lucca aka Joseph Luccis aka *"Jumbo"* aka *"Giambone"*.

i

THE STORY

CHAPTER 1

"Lino, I can't hold it in anymore!" implored agonized little, curly-red-haired Giuseppe Rossi with increasing urgency, holding the front of his thick brown woolen pants scrunched up and jumping around from foot-to-foot between the grazing goats.

His face was contorted in a form of pain.

"By the Holy Virgin, Pèppe! C'mon!"

commanded his by two year's older cousin Pasqualino Acquaviva, holding the family's gentle gray donkey, Lisetta, by the bridle with one hand and a homemade wooden rod -- a goatherd's crook -- in the other.

"You can do your business back here behind the olive trees and scrub bushes."

Pèppe scrambled as best he could to the small secluded clearing Lino had indicated, between the nanny, billy, and kid goats nibbling around at its edges.

Still slightly pudgy but compact, just-turned-four-year-old Pèppe checked first that the coast was clear, unbuckled the suspenders of his serge knicker-bockers, hunkered down, and took the position one does in the outdoors to relieve oneself.

The tinkling sound of a welcome rivulet followed.

Other sounds, like muffled explosionettes from a miniature machine-gun, undertoned the episode.

The lads always had some old newsprint or scraps of rough wrap paper with them for just these urgent situations. Such niceties, however, were still scarce.

In a pinch, even a leaf would do…but *not* those stinging-nettles!

Pasqualino realized that he, too, should listen to the call of nature, but not wanting to seem as beholden to his bodily functions as his little cousin, discreetly, nonchalantly moved behind a small oak, with obedient, docile Lisetta blocking the view to the goat-clearing and dependent little Giuseppe.

The older of the two cousins only had to pass water, luckily for his honor.

Upon finishing up, giving the last shake, Lino spied something out of the periphery of his vision:

a goat, a smallish goat, yes, but piebald;

… his parent's and his Nonni's animals were either one predominant color or two at most, but certainly not splotched with black and brown and mixed spots on a white background.

In the meantime, Giuseppe had returned and followed his older cousin's gaze to where the variegated kid was nibbling on some grass and shrubs.

Animals were like a magnet to this little boy, particularly the younger ones, and he was drawn almost immediately to this endearing little critter -- the instant his vision and perception locked focus on the grazing kid, the likes of which he had never seen before.

Pèppe had no fear of creatures either great or small.

In an instant, he had gone over and was bending down, petting and then embracing the newcomer around the neck.

They became instant *amici*.

Their herd's proud, jealous queen, a beautiful russet brown, almost like Giuseppe's hair, noticed the intruder and began approaching it with quickening steps, followed by her own two kids — one of which was colored that special brown like her; the other, half-white and half-black like the father -- that had been born in March; now in late May, the scions of her herd were not yet weaned, but already bellicose toward encroaching strangers.

From the other side, the old buck, the royal children's father, began accelerating up from the far end of the herd, at the lower corner of the clearing sloping down the mountain, head down, butting position ready.

Lino observed all of this happening – he was not a bad goatherd even for his young years, but was on the wrong side of Lisetta to intervene in time with his goatherd's stick, made by his Zio Donato, the lads' Nonna Domenica's brother, from the gnarled roots and strong thin trunk of a dried sapling olive.

The top of Lino's rod was cross-shaped, but with a ram's head gazing bravely out from the polished and varnished roots, at the intersection of the cross's vertical and horizontal beams, now the top of his staff.

Through this amassing confusion, almost imperceptibly, in the background of his consciousness, the older cousin thought he heard what sounded like an accelerating crescendo of rumbling thunder and a metallic rattling.

Beginning to panic now, his body tensing, Pasqualino knew he couldn't stop what seemed like an imminent catastrophe....

******

CHAPTER 2

The path beyond the cemetery was the one all the families used to climb up the barely three-meter-wide, limestone gravelled path that weaved and wove and climbed its way up Mount Chianiello.

Sometimes, to gather wood, Pasqualino's Mamma, Teresa Salerno *in Acquaviva,* would continue through and along these ways all the way to Capizzo and Magliano Vetere, making the trip several times a week, indeed almost every day.

Sunday was reserved, however, only for social visits to her beloved brother and sister-in-law in Magliano. No heavy-laden baskets balanced on her head on the day of resting.

But Sunday was the only day of respite, and sometimes only in the afternoon....

Teresa's burdens were the wealth and treasures produced by the mountain and its people:
chestnuts, wood, olives, olive oil, stones for kilning into limestone, grapes, wine, tobacco leaves, an occasional flower when she had the brief leisure to consider Nature's splendor.

Usually she carried these loads in large, roughly-woven wicker baskets on her head, sometimes doing two trips a day, but at times Teresa Acquaviva would have Lisetta accompany her, especially when she had to carry a particularly lot of heavy things such as rocks or firewood, saddling the gentle donkey with a *bisaccia*, a double-sacked pack-saddle especially designed for the beasts of burden.

Always faster than the other women, she walked proudly, head held high, aware of her beauty. She took especial care of her simple dresses to make the most of them.

Having Lisetta to assist her in no way relieved the young, Grecian-looking mother from her own onus of balancing additional sylvan resources on her head!

Both "creatures" were laden, both involved in the work, both involved in the duties of nourishing hearth, home, and herds.

The bare-rock summit of Monte Chianiello was at a little over 1'300 meters high, 700 meters above their village of Monteforte.

There was a distinct, wide, petrous-gray swath at the very top; lower down a brownish-gray one; then the dark greens of the forests above, at, and below the village.

Over the eons, 7 or 8 ravines had been scratched down into the mountain's side, all aiming at the village like the center of a gargantuan geographical target.

Of extremely ancient origins, this small village of Monteforte Cilento has a layout and an architecture belying its former purpose as a medieval fortification --

-- so much so that those who dare venture down the narrow lanes and alleys of the old town can still discover what remains of the arches, walls, and steps of the ancient castle, whose ruins, over the years, have been completely incorporated into the village.

Monteforte seems to cascade down the very side of the lower reaches of Mount Chianiello, in a shower of brown-ocher fired clay roof tiles, like the scaley armor of an immense, resting red dragon.

In those latter days of the Second World War, about 1'000 souls carried on the threads of their births, lives, and deaths in Monteforte Cilento.

From the ancient courtyard at the top part of the village – *"la Piazza"* -- the town square – the former old entrance gates now correspond to the current points of road accesses.

In the historical heart of Monteforte, further down the winding, serpentine steps leading, again, from the Piazza above, the architecture is characterized by the typical compact "town-fabric" layout that arises organically in such European villages, around the medieval squares surrounding the multiple and various churches:

The Church of San Pietro; The Church of Santa Maria dell' Assunta; The Chapel of San Donato, the youthful-looking Patron Saint of Monteforte; The Chapel of the Madonna dell'Autuori; and The Chapel of the Madonna delle Grazie.

Why so many chapels and churches for such a small village?

Was it a shadow, a re-packaging of the ancient pagan deities of the pantheons that had held sway over these regions for millennia?

Or did the townsfolk of this remote fortress need an especially large amount of protective saints and piety to hold in check their strong human passions, drives, and appetites?

Or both?

Legend has it that there had been multiple sightings and visitations of Our Lady at these very points in the geography of Monteforte Cilento, turning them into sacred ground, deserving of monuments to the Madonna and the Saints.

In addition to the holy edifices, there are also stately residences, various *Palazzi,* to be marveled at in Monteforte.

For example, from the sixteenth century there are the Palazzo Cartolano and the Palazzo Baronale. In this latter, the remains of the old prisons are still visible. From the eighteenth-century there are the Palazzo Forte and the Palazzo Gorga, the Palazzo Capozzoli, and the Palazzo Cerulli and Scavarone.

The name *"Monteforte"* derives from *Mons Fortis,* which means a "fortified height or hill".

It, indeed, had once been a Roman *"castrum"*, i.e., a military fortress, as well as a *"castellum"*, or a place inhabited by civilians but included within a fortified enclosure.

It was the Lombards and later the Normans who expanded and made the Castle-controlled areas safer.

In the Middle Ages, Monteforte was one of the outposts of the state of *"Baronia dei Novi"*.

In 1144 it became the possession of a Norman Knight Henry – possibly from the village of Monteforte itself, under King Roger, at which time it was already known as Monteforte.

Later, in 1463, the King of Naples, Ferdinand of Aragon, granted the possession of Monteforte to Barbarino Roberto De Finicolo and the Sanseverino family, princes of Salerno.

Thereafter, it was bequeathed to Bartolomeo Del Mercato.

Much later, in 1700, it became the property of the Spanish noble family Ziches.

What of the language of the regular townspeople, of the poorer, uneducated classes, who did not have a Palazzo as their domicile and *"paesani"* to do their menial work for them?

If one expects to be able to speak and understand Italian here, one would be sorely mistaken.

Because of the invasions by various and sundry peoples into this *Mezzogiorno* of Southern Italy -- into Campania, into the Cilento, into Monteforte itself, and because of the numerous changes of the nationalities of those in power, the Latin-based language spoken there was transformed into a dialect almost unintelligible to the High-Italian speakers, whose tongue was based on Dante Alighieri's Florentine.

The dialects vary and change, even from village to village, with local idiolects making the character and cadence of these towns idiosyncratic, culturally unique.

******

The population continually suffered from the vagaries of alternating fortunes, the impacts of the proud plans of men and the whims of nature and fate.

In 1340, the village was ravished by the plague, while the sixteenth century saw significant resurgence in the growth of population and trade.

In 1656, the grim visitation, once again, of the plague decimated the population anew, but the following century witnessed a rebirth of the center of Monteforte, with the construction of new buildings, better economic prosperity, and the expansion of the town.

From an administrative point of view, from 1811 to 1860 Monteforte was part of the district of Gioi, in the District of Vallo of the Kingdom of the Two Sicilies.

During the Kingdom of Italy it was part of the mandate of Gioi, of the district of Vallo della Lucania.

But the history of Monteforte is further linked to one of the most important pages in the history of the unification of Italy: the *Risorgimento*.

The notorious Capozzoli brothers, both heroes and brigands, were born and lived here.[1] Their legacy is controversial, at best....

****

The flora is beautiful there on the slopes of Mount Chianiello.

Aleppo pine, oaks, laurels, and beeches, massive, gnarled, ancient chestnuts, the occasional wild cherry, mountain flowers comprised the plant variety of this mountainous Mediterranean region.

Pines, however, preferred the lower regions nearer the shore, near Paestum, but the occasional scrub variety could be found on the lower flanks of Chianiello's slopes.

---

[1] http://www.montefortemultimedia.it/

Some wild pigs, otters, voles, weasels, foxes, mice, wild rabbits, an occasional wolf made up only some of the members of the local fauna.

Below the village, in the moister, more accessible regions of the mountain's foot areas, the families were already starting to revive, re-cultivate their olive and medlar orchards and wine-grape vine-yards, after the upheavals of the war and the shifting forces of alliance and occupation – previously German, now allied American and British.

Normalcy had begun to make its tenuous, fragile return as the front lines in this second global war had been pushed further and further North, toward the Teutonic heartland.

It was late May 1944.

Pasqualino's father, Annunziante Acquaviva, was still fighting with the "new" Allies against Italy's former "Allies". Monte Cassino would be reconquered that very month.

The temperature was cool now in mid-spring and its still not yet infrequent rain showers, with the gently rising temperatures of the coming summer heat approaching at an increasing speed.

Minor tributaries to the Fiume Alento went down the ravines during this "rainy" season, most drying completely by mid-summer.

In the area, too, further afield, there were other rivers with such magical names as *"il Fiume Calore"* and *"il Fiume Mingardo"*.

The vegetation was flourishing at this time of year, and it was a chance to fatten up the herds and the beasts of burden such as Lisetta and the goats, after winter's dearth.

Bees and insects, including butterflies and flies and beetles and mosquitoes and ticks kept the boys attentive and on their guard – simultaneously to the responsibilities of guarding the herd.

****

CHAPTER 3

"Watch out, Pèppe!", Pasqualino shouted out in dire warning.

Releasing the piebald goatlet and simultaneously turning toward his elder cousin's voice, Giuseppe's eyes saw the aggressive buck rapidly approaching up from one end of the large clearing – he didn't see the nanny and her twins nearing him, albeit more slowly than the buck, from the other point of the triangulation.

Reflexively, Giuseppe stood up – there was not much of him – and backed into a too shallow nook in a diminutive mountain boulder above which grew, was just barely thriving, a scraggly pine tree; the small varicolored kid scampered now up onto this boulder, above and behind Giuseppe's head, to the safety of this miniature promontory.

Calm and nonchalant stood the little goat, observing the scene below him like a proud patrician spectator at the Roman Colosseum, giving an occasional comment in the form of a high-pitched bleat.

Closing his eyes, red-haired Giuseppe tried to scrunch himself as best he could away from the coming crush; Lino now having maneuvered himself past Lisetta, ramming staff in hand, yelling, still 20 meters away.

"WHOOMP!"
and woody, pre-splintering creaks, metallic rattles.

Giuseppe wasn't sure what had happened… luckily, he had gone to the bathroom just before.

Fully opening his eyes from the closed squinch of fear they had been in, all was suddenly quiet, but for the bleating-braying of the imperial twins and the loud protestations of their ram-buck father.

A large, human-shaped shadow shielding the boy from the sun in his stony crevvy.

The image that came into focus was wearing some sort of a low cap and cloak and a formerly dark, now age-faded, red bandana.

Pasqualino rushed in at that moment to add to Giuseppe's mustering defenses and inspect the physical integrity and soundness of the small child-package put into his care by his mother and beloved aunt.

"Pèppe, Pèppe! Are you hurt? Are you hurt?"

As was his wont and his character, like the carefree nature of the goats he loved after facing and surviving potentially mortal danger, curly-red-topped Giuseppe did not respond to his cousin's concerns, but rather simply got himself out of his miniature mountain crevice sanctuary and went closer to the large image, now totally curious, seemingly having completely forgotten the precarious predicament he had been in just seconds before.

"Who are you, Sir?"
-- inquired the precocious, doughty little lad.

To the children, he appeared to be ancient, about 100 or more, the shape before them coalescing into what seemed a powerful hermit or a muscular mountain gnome – perhaps just over one-and-a-half meters tall.

A short-brimmed dark-dark brown woolen cap or beret on his pate, low over his eyes.

A long brown, heavy-fabricked trench coat or overcoat, slung over his shoulders like a cloak, covered a rough-woolen sweater and brown leather suspenders.

Where had he come from?

He seemed to have materialized out of the forest itself.

A heavy goatherd's crook was in his left hand, the top was a horned dragon and the curved crook itself was its tail, in old hard dark and blackened, lovingly carved wood.

With his crook, the stranger had hooked the horns of the billy-buck and had turned it, forced it, to the ground, after it had butted the side of a one-by-two meter grayed-wood-plank cart on mid-sized wide metal hooved, wooden-spoked wheels.

The animal was down on the knees of its forelegs, pinned to the ground, and was kicking up the gravel of the path with its hind ones – complaining in loud protest at this indignity.

Although old and short, the man's chest was barrel-built and his arms and legs tightened and filled the cloth of the coat and heavy woolen trousers snugly.

A powerfully built, timeless old troll.

The queen and her kids had decided it was better not to approach and had moved away to nibble on some tufts of wiry mountain grass.

Pasqualino had by now moved close to his cousin and was diagonally to his side, protecting him, all the while watching this strange scene –

… their dominant male goat, braying and held flailing helplessly on the ground, whereupon the strange old man suddenly released his hircine captive and moved aggressively in its direction to scare it away, asserting his dominance.

Shaking its coat and its goatee, its horns, its fore- and back-legs, it moved back to the herd after spitting out one last disparaging bleat, still wobbling a bit at first, and began chewing some grass, no longer the slightest indication of hurt pride or apparent remembrance of what had just transpired.

The man turned away from the boys, reached up, and took down his wayward buckling, whispered something tenderly in its ear, and then placed it and tied it inside his cart on a blanket, next to his staff, giving it some dandelions to occupy itself with.

Silent still toward his fellow beings, seemingly not even aware of them, he began walking back, further up the path toward the secrecy of the forest from which he had appeared, pulling the cart with the t-shaped tug-shaft, between the trees, entering the small, shallow gorge where a tributary rivulet of the Alento ran.

Almost angry now at being ignored, Giuseppe ran a short way toward this their mysterious savior and called out defiantly to his receding back,

"Who are you, Sir? Tell us!"

Pasqualino was amazed and somewhat shocked at the audacity of his little cousin and afraid of the consequences of a young one being so brash and demanding of an elder in this culture of filial obedience.

The cart with its content of one small variegated goat and a blanket stopped abruptly at the end of the clearing, before the light-graveled path entered the way to the ravine.

The lads held their breath, their bodies tensed.

Putting down the pull handle, the aged stranger turned back, slowly but determinedly, to face the direction from which he had left the boys. As he passed the side flank of his wooden cart, the old man patted the head of the by-now quietened goat and strode toward the little red-head.

He looked down at the boy, almost seemed to smile, patted him as he had done the goat, then looked over Pèppe's head at Pasqualino.

A few moments of taut silence passed, then…

"Who made your crook?" he asked the older child, voice low and deep, but clearly, in high Italian, with no indication of the Campanian accent.

"My Zio Donato," answered Pasqualino Acquaviva hesitatingly in the respectful tone he had learned from his parents and grandparents, a bit taken aback by the unexpected question.

"Which Donato?
There are so many in Monteforte;
almost one in every family,"
inquired the mountain-man.

"Donato D'Orsi, Signore."

The elderly man paused a mere moment, his eyes widening briefly, then crossed his arms and put his hand under his clean-shaven chin.

He looked up and away into the sky, then returned his crinkled gaze back toward Lino, then toward Giuseppe, eyes narrowed slightly.

"Not the woodworker, the big carpenter? The brother of Domenica and Antonio?"

"Yes, sir. My Nonna Domenica's brother....

He makes these crooks from the trunks and roots of trees; that's my Zio Donato."

As wind-whipped clouds fleetingly, darkly shadow the sun and then pass as soon as they had come, so did something cross over the old man's visage; briefly he gazed back over his shoulder at the ornate dragon-headed crook lying next to the resting goatlet in the bed of the simple cart

Then he turned back, passed Giuseppe and was now standing diagonally and between the boys so he and they could see each other directly, alternating his attention between them, a twinkling seriousness returned to his demeanor....

"Tell that old Bear that the 'Giambone' sends his greetings."

Having said this the old man walked back to his cart; passing Giuseppe, he put some almonds and two dried figs into his chubby, freckled little hands.

******

CHAPTER 4

Sitting and enjoying the delectable sweetmeats the *Giambone* had given them, later in the day as a *merendina*, now up on the rock where the little piebald kid goat had been, in the shade of the scraggly pine, Giuseppe eating some yellow raspberries to supplement them, both children not saying anything, looking up now and again to ascertain that the goats in their charge were still safe and sound.

Pasqualino rises, begins walking a bit, kicking – almost absentmindedly – little unseen somethings in the grasses, finally formulates into word the conclusions of his cogitations:

"Pèppe, tomorrow, when we come back, let's bring Lisetta to the little ravine, just past the clearing, into the forest...I'm sure there are some tasty plants and flowers, that, perhaps, we can later feed to our caprette...."

"Mamma and Papá will thank us because the milk and cheese will certainly be much tastier!"

"Yes, Lino! And perhaps we might even find some frogs and fish in the little brook!" said Giuseppe.

With this plan now forged, and their anticipation for the coming day filling their spirits, the little goat-herding Davids shepherded the flock back down to the protection of their families' shed in Monteforte and then off to dinner at their respective homes they went, at the Acquaviva's and the Rossi's.

It was just as well that they didn't need to tell their parents of their adventures – both hungry and tired, they devoured their dinners of *pasta e fave* with *freselle* – *"viscuotti"* in their dialect -- of whole grain, watered-down homemade wine to drink, some goat's milk espressi as post-prandials, before they were shuffled off to bed by their mothers and nonnas.

******

CHAPTER 5

Zia Teresa, Pasqualino's mother, was surprised to see Giuseppe at her heavy wooden, black-iron-strap-braced door much earlier than usual.

That previous evening he had slept at his own home, across the common yard, which was his habit only about half the evenings of a given week. Usually, he overnighted with his older cousin as the two were closer in age than Giuseppe's older siblings.

As was his right as one of the family, he entered without knocking, but politely said, *"Permesso"*.

Even more strange was that Pasqualino was ready too, having had his breakfast of some more dried *viscuotti* with his weakened, child-concentration coffee and milk.

"Did the goat's ask you to come so early?",
Mamma inquired impishly, eyes twinkling.

Not getting an immediate answer, she put her
fists on her hips and interrogated directly:

"What are you two up to?" putting her trained
suspicions into a question...she sensed an unusual
eagerness in the boys' willingness to get started.

Pasqualino took the hardened goatmilk ricotta
cheese and the dried spicy salami his Mamma had
packed for the two of them, and some worn-by-age-
and-use, ceramic-capped, ceramic-bodied bottles of
water.

She knew that they would supplement their
lunches with the berries and figs ladening the
bushes and trees on the mountain at this time of
year.

The morning was cool and vernal and with only
some wispy clouds, aeolian hair filaments and
strands lazily passing overhead. She wasn't worried
about their safety, but something piqued her
mother's intuition.

"Well, in a way...,"

Lino began to reply, dodgingly, to the first question that his mother had posed -- actually _not_ to him but to her curly-red-haired nephew --, not looking at her directly, but giving the appearance of being busy by making sure that the cloth packsack across little Giuseppe's front and side was properly closed and sitting well.

Pasqualino Acquaviva had already been weaned on his culture's ancient knowledge that the best way to cover a secret plan was to describe it as near to the truth as possible.

Just a *slightly* little mendacious tale...but *mostly* true, well *partly* true, well *somewhat almost true....*

"We saw some nice green pastures just a bit further up the mountain, on the other side of the clearing, with dandelions and clover and green bushes...very good for the goats and their milk, Mamma."

"Oh, I see," replied Mamma looking at the two of them fixedly, suspiciously, still not convinced.

After all, she had grown up in Monteforte, too.

"But don't go <u>too</u> far up that trail, higher up, further up the ravine. And be careful at the brook…don't cross it. It's not too swollen with water now, but…

"Lino….?!"

Pasqualino had now gotten himself ready and was assertively pulling the little Giuseppe out the door.

At Mamma's question, he thought it better to turn around obediently and reply,

"Yes, Mamma, I know. We are always careful. Papá and you and Zio have shown us the way many times, and Giuseppe's brothers and sisters are with their herds at the higher clearing."

A last vestige of uncertainty remained in her mother's intuitive heart; finally, she granted her boys the benefit of the doubt, trusted her boys – she had really little other choice in these difficult times -- and gave them both a peck on the tops of their heads and sent them off.

Out the door they now went, Lino letting out a surreptitious breath of relief, unnoticed by the others, as he departed out, over the threshold, the unspoken blessing of maternal care and concern following them from Mamma's eyes and heart like a guardian angel, a hidden companion with a sword of protection.

She went back to cleaning the house and preparing the family's laundry to wash at the fountain on the Piazza.

Later that morning, she would make her way up the path across Monte Chianiello, skirting below its ridge that looked like the vertebrae on a backbone of some huge slumbering dragon-beast, past the even smaller-than-Monteforte village of Capizzo to her sister-in-law Elena's home in Magliano Vetere, to pay a brief unexpected call.

On her way, she would check to see how the boys were doing with their goats....

****

CHAPTER 6

The goats were waiting for Lino and Pèppe in their home pens, seemingly especially excited that morning – either because they smelled the aromas of the fresh mountain shrubs, the low hanging branches of figs, of brambles and berries and other trees, and dandelions and thistles and grasses and forbs in the air, anticipating munching on them, the mountain vegetation;

Or, perhaps, despite the apparent aggression of it all, they had enjoyed that pulse-raising episode of the previous day with the mysterious old man, his cart, and his multicolored, wayward kid;

Or perhaps both … and others, for humanly incomprehensible reasons.

Whatever it was, the lads -- leading Lisetta on a worn leather tether -- and their herd were gamboling particularly frisky and efficient on that early-June morn on the laps of Monte Chianiello.

In a little more than half an hour, they had ascended and arrived at their herd's clearing.

In the distance, further up the path from where the mysterious stranger had appeared yesterday to save them, all was still silent, only a few small flying insects circling lazily in the sunlit air – Lino and Pèppe were already there even before Giuseppe's elder siblings would come by with their mixed herd of goats and sheep.

The duo of lads still had some few almonds and a single dried fig that the *"Giambone"* had given them the day before, that brought back to their young minds the memory-images of the adventure of yesterday and its rescuing, unfathomable hero; and nibbled on these last friands while they sat on the small outcropping boulder below the insouciant emaciated juvenile pine where his young goat had imperiously stood the day before.

"*Pèppe,*" Pasqualino began, sending child-sized, palatable tidbits of his plan to his "immature" cousin:

"*Mamma will be coming by in about an hour, maybe a little more. We are going to wait here and tend the goats until Mamma comes by...OK?*"

"*Yes, Lino, I know that already.*"

"*And before that, very soon, your brothers and sisters will be coming by with their herds....*"

"*Yes, I know that, too. They do that every day, even on Sunday after mass...just like we do, Lino.*"

"*Good, Pèppe, very good.*"

Little Giuseppe had just turned 4 – "*You are now in your 5th year,*" as Nonna Domenica always said -- earlier that month, but something made him uneasy about this way in which his older cousin was conversing with him, almost at him, as if saying something, but not saying it.

A light twinge of fear rippled through his still slightly baby-chub stomach and loins, but he was yet too young to put it into words…he simply ate more quickly.

This would not be the first time Lino had put them into a difficult position….

******

CHAPTER 7

In the dependable human gearworks of these regions with few physical clocks and even fewer watches, the Rossi's herd passed Pasqualino and Giuseppe, as expected, shepherded by the little boy's older brothers and sisters, with the older male fraternal twin, Domenico, throwing fallen, weathered pinecones from last autumn at them, and Domenico's fraternal-twin sister, Francesca, grabbing Giuseppe up like a rag doll and kissing and tickling him under the neck while blowing false flatulence sounds under his chubby cheeks, on his neck, while he giggled and squirmed uncontrollably;

the eldest girl and boy – Emilia and Vittorio -- continued on responsibly, aware of their duties, with the herd.

A girl, then a boy, then twins – a girl and a boy, and then a few years later Giuseppe had come as a delighting surprise.

The elder Rossi children continued onwards, on to their pastures further up the path, after they had "tormented" their little brother and cousin enough.

Lino always tried to remain calm and collected and coolly proud in the face of his elder cousins' taunting, teasing, and rough-house tickling; only infrequently was he successful.

Pasqualino and Giuseppe continued their conscientious guarding of their grazing area, the "danger" of the cousins now past, having moved further up the path keeping to the right of the rivulet brook, a tributary of the Alento, snaking along with it until they reached the Rossi's clearing and pastures, after a small bosky area.

After that point, beyond the older siblings' grazing area, the path continued on until it broke off and away from the rivulet and veered again to the right toward Capizzo and even further on to Magliano Vetere.

This was Teresa Aquaviva's daily trail.

After the approximately predicted one-and-a-bit hours, Mamma came up the road, on her head a large glass-flask, dark green, full of olive oil from last November's meagre gathering, the first relatively peaceful harvest of the waning war, the bulbous lower part of the thick glass bottle wrapped with woven wicker, like a rough home-knit sweater with handles around a squat obese dwarf. A fat cork stopper kept the precious golden fluid safe inside.

To keep her long thick black Graecian locks under control and to follow the ways of their traditional modesty, Mamma was wearing a faded, dark-blue handkerchief on her head.

A cloth towel, rolled up and rounded into the shape of a tight *taralle,* helped to keep balance to her transports as well as ease the weight of the olive-oil glass amphora.

The week's laundry was washed and drying at Nonna Domenica's home – she did her own, plus helped with her parents' and her in-law's linens and clothes.

Pèppe and Lino were at the far end of the pasture, slightly below the path amongst the small boulders and grasses when Mamma passed.

Pèppe was picking dandelions and feeding the smaller goat-kids from a bouquet-bundle he held in his hand, while Lino was kicking a large pinecone through the grass, occasionally hitting it with the long staff of his crook.

Relieved, finally, to see them playing and at their duties, despite her forebodings, she simply called to them and waved with one hand while balancing the load on her head with the other and continued on to Elena, her sister-in-law, and her brother Luigi in Magliano Vetere.

She would spend time with them, coffee and some small sweetbits, perhaps a confetto or dried figs stuffed with almonds or walnut and fennel insides and then return with eggs, some salami, and tobacco leaves for her father, Nonno Francesco Salerno, and her father-in-law Pasquale Acquaviva.

Her husband Annunziante – *"Nunzio"* was still with Italy's new Allies and their troops after joining them the previous year...

… and he was still safe, as far as she knew, according to the ardent letter Teresa had received two weeks before….

Pasqualino was their only child thus far, named as was tradition, after her father-in-law, her husband Nunzio's father, *Pasquale*.

****

Pasqualino had his fox-kit-eyes raptor-fixed on Mamma's back as he and Giuseppe waved to her, she disappearing straight-backed, proud on into the forest.

She went this way several times a week, sometimes twice a day — at times to family, at other times to collect wood for burning or charcoal or sometimes even for *"pietre vive"* -- used for making lime for building and re-building, stones fire-roasted in the special heating kilns down below the village until they were reduced to a white powder essential for cement and mortar. Fall brought with it the chestnut harvests.

The mountain was not dead to the Montefortese, but was like a living, breathing, vital mother protecting and feeding them, giving them both physical and aesthetic delights.

Trouble, too, at times …

… there would be an occasional small rockfall or a seismic tremor now and then, but the mountains were old and had reached a mature, relative stability that kept them mostly benignant even during the larger earthquakes.

Once Mamma had been gone a safe time and distance, Lino's vulpine trickiness whisked away his innocence, and he sprang into goal-directed action.

From beyond the rim-edge of the clearing behind him, just where the forest was beginning again, he brought forth two long sticks, about 2 meters each and began fastening them together with some rough hemp twine he had brought with him.

"Are we going to play church…to pray, Lino?
Tomorrow is mass with Padre Massimiliano…
Can I serve the holy 'ostie'?"

… asked the little red-head as he watched his companion sct up what seemed to be a cross.

Pasqualino was tamping the rough, woodland crucifix into the ground above the clearing, in front of their rock-station, but below the path, with a fist-sized stone.

"We are …<stone-banging and puffing>… *going to make … a guardian … for our goats, Peppino,"* he said, puffing a bit between the hammerings and slightly grunting, exhaling at the effort of standing on a small boulder and beating the vertical mast of the cross into the ground.

From his cloth pouch, he took out one of his Papá's old fieldwork shirts and a worn beret from his Nonno Pasquale.

He tied some of his twine around the midriff of the shirt, stuffed some dry grasses in to puff out the chest and buttoned it up closed.

Then, he put a wooden shingle with an angry face on it, drawn in charcoal, below the beret and within the collar of the shirt;

This, too, he fastened with the twine.

Old worn leather working gloves -- filled, too, with field grass -- from his Nonno Francesco were slipped on at the distal opposite points of the horizontal beam.

Finally, a rough staff was leaned against "his" right hand; Lino was keeping his.

"A 'spaventapasseri' !!!!!!"

Pèppe squealed in delight and began hopping and gamboling below the figure, some goat-kids following him to greedily eat up the delectable dandelions and wildflowers he was losing unconcernedly from his bouquet.

"Yes, our guardian scarecrow. 'Michele' will watch the goats and keep them safe from foxes and wolves, my little Cousin. He is our guardian and helper, and I put my rosary around his neck for extract protection by the Virgin."

"Now let's have a little merendina, Pèppe."

****

CHAPTER 8

Saying nothing, but looking down and kicking the stones on the path hugging the Alento brook heading deeper and deeper into the forest, Giuseppe followed his older cousin a few paces behind, not quite dragging his feet, but almost.

…Lisetta with them, in case Giuseppe became too tired and-or cranky.

At the right bend toward Capizzo and the Rossi sibling's pasture clearing further along, still out of sight, Lino took his cousin's hand and veered left, at a point where even Pèppe could just spy what seemed like a narrow track for wild animals, the foliage slightly beaten down in two almost invisible parallel tracks, leading to the small brook and then, across it, toward the gradually rising vegetated wall of the ravine.

The hard rock splinters and gravel that journeyers and invaders from various sides and loyalties had laid down on top of what the residents had placed down over the long history of Monteforte and this region, made any possible tracks of the Giambone's goat-cart practically invisible.

****

Lisetta went on ahead of them, following what for the boys were barely visible signs through the light foresty area. Perhaps, too, following aromas and scents that only her species was acutely attuned to.

Sometimes the cousins Pasqualino and Giuseppe spotted the round, dark black-green pellet goat droppings and then, just a few meters away from a low fordable area of the stream, a larger pile of what they recognized as donkey manure.

They had never been in this area before, but they sensed that they were approaching something "special".

The boys continued to follow this woodland path, made of barely visible tracks and traces and droppings, just behind Lisetta, who now and then stopped to chomp delicately on one of the delectable mountain flowering plants amongst the low-growing vegetation, then over some flat stones of the creek across to the other side and up into the forest, when she and the boys spy something, just a bit beyond this shallow ford, on the other banklet of the brook, that looks like a beehive, nearly a meter tall.

The boys stop at this almost invisible brown clay "thing", overgrown, but not totally covered, by a possessive, colonizing vine.

It is close to eye-level for Pasqualino;

Giuseppe needs to look up to see its ever-so slightly-flattened, round top.

Reminiscent to them of a hive, or perhaps a *"nuraghe"* of Sardinia, if they had only known of such things in this remote mountain area of the Mezzogiorno.

At the very top of the structure, below an overhanging clay flap like an eyelid, is an empty opening in the stylized almond shape of a wide-open, empty eye – gazing blindly away and up.

Their own eyes are drawn hypnotically, almost unconsciously, by this "eye" in the direction of another "hivelet", not more than twenty meters further away, up the sloping mountainside.

Going up the trail, another one of the domelets meets them; this one contains a homemade suet-based candle, now burned out, within the larger opening at the base; again a smaller, clay-eyelid - covered, almond-shaped opening at the top, this dark, empty "eye" staring in the direction of the next miniature "*nuraghe*", the next hive, another 20 meters away again.

The "eyes" seem to mesmerize and lead them on…toward what?

The children are silent as they walk. Only the late-spring twitterings and buzzings of the forest, the diminishing burblings of the brook audible.

Lisetta, too, seems to be especially quiet and respectful.

The "hives" blend in with the mountain stones.

Some of these latter, ancient boulders are almost completely earth and moss-covered, settled where they were deposited, over the eons, and one would not even notice the odd, man-made domed structures amongst them if you didn't know that they were there.

Yet another miniature dome contains a rough-woven cross, formed into the iconic Christian symbol by long, flexible twigs.

Their various coverings of dried clay-mud, or ivy foliage, or stuck-in reeds and leaves and pinecones camouflage them.

The hidden path has become more noticeable now, and had begun a gradual, winding way, up the hill, always moving them in the direction of the next nuraghe, up the mountain's sloping flank.

Different forms, some clay, some woven, some made by tiny stones mortared together, but all in generally the same shape and more or less the same size, not all with a slightly flat top, but all with an eye facing on to the next structure, finally up to a small waterfall that had been completely unnotice-able to the children from the path further below.

From where they are, the burbling sound of the fall's water is increasing in volume.

Little Giuseppe has bunched tight the crotch of his heavy trousers and is now less walking than jigging along the path behind Pasqualino.

The elder cousin seems to be almost entranced as he moves up the trail behind Lisetta, drawn, pulled to the next nuraghetta.

"*Lino!*" the little boy finally blurts out,
"*we need to return to the goats now.
I'm getting afraid, and I have to make a pee!*"

Stopped in his movement to pursue the tracks, as if snapped back out of a hypnosis, Pasqualino slows down, and shakes his head to clear his mind.

He hesitates, considering now the location of the
sun, the slowly, but ineluctably lengthening
shadows, and then, almost reluctantly, he whistled
to Lisetta, took her harness and returned to little
Giuseppe.

*"It's good, Pèppe. Let's go back to our goats and Michele.
Come now. We can return another day. Go to the bathroom
here, behind this bush while I hold Lisetta still to shield
you,"* the older boy comforts soothingly with his
voice to his younger charge.

He did not want to stretch Pèppe's willingness to
the breaking point.

Giuseppe scoots behind the temporary privy his
cousin had made for him and mercifully relieves
himself.

As is always the case, the way back to their
clearing would be much faster than their path to
this point just across the brook, the tiny tribulet.

To further fix the loyalty of his little ally,
Pasqualino put Giuseppe on top of Lisetta for the
ride back home, to the little cousin's delight.

A small bit of salami was ready as a snack for the chubby redhead's voyage.

One-by-one they passed these mysterious structures on their descent down the hidden trail.

Neither of them would soon forget the little "hives" – as they considered them -- they had seen; their curiosities were piqued to continue on.

The next day would be faster…and Mamma would be leaving just after church to spend most of her Sunday in Magliano Vetere: on that day less for toil than for pleasure, with her brother's family.

****

Back at the goats, all is well, with just one kid entangled in some spiny, thorny brambles, but nothing else of note.

The middays are becoming warmer and warmer as spring changes into the Cilento summer with its *Sole Leone* –the hot, dry, intense Leonine Sun.

It is late mid-afternoon and soon the Rossi herd would be returning from the upper pastures and Pasqualino and Giuseppe's small cloven-hooved troupe would join them for the trip back down the mountain.

The boys dismantle and hide their Guardian Archangel Michele – now having proven his mettle, on this his maiden mission with his hircine legions, against the infernal dangers that could befall them – and prepare to return the herd to their corral and home stalls in Monteforte Cilento.

Mamma would return not much later in the day.

****

Frank A. Merola

CHAPTER 9

That evening, Lino and Pèppe both stay at Nonna Domenica's.

Even though just across the common central yard-area of their encircling homes, Mamma would be spending the night with her sister Filomena and her husband, Mauro, and Giuseppe's older siblings.

The two boys are inseparable, and Giuseppe's mother, Filomena, is Teresa's sister, and knows how much the little lads enjoy their times with their beloved Nonna Domenica.

Domenica and her husband's, Francesco's, place shares a wall with the Acquavivas' and is across the small grassy area from the Rossis', the little yard where the animals' stalls and the chickens are.

They are now also fortunate enough to have a new, additional, young piglet swine.

A massive old chestnut is in the center with a few lemon trees, medlars, cactuses, and some aglianico grapevines creating a shady arbor.

It is actually like one big home – a farmstead, a *fattoria* -- spread across this small interconnected area. Thus, a parent or relative or a sibling is always nearby.

Nonna Domenica prepares them a simple but delicious dinner – minestra made from tender dandelion leaves, mixed with olive oil, garlic, and some salt, and *viscuotti* – and later tells them stories after they've sipped their little espressi made child-safe by being thinned out with goatmilk.

Nonno Francesco normally leaves after dinner for some *Strega* and increasingly available, locally grown and rolled cigarettes, and freer, wide-ranging discussions at the *"Bar Salerno"* – commemorating, amongst other topics, the successful landings from Operation Avalanche of the Americans and the Allies at the beachheads in Paestum and in Salerno.

****

The Bar is ideally located, up at the *Piazza*, with a breathtaking view of the cascading orange-red baked-clay tiles of the homes and churches of Monteforte and, further down and away, of the *Alento* valley and the *Piana della Rocca*.

It had always been a popular locale for the male citizenry of the village and belonged to one of Francesco's elder brothers and a sister.

Allied units had only recently cleared out German resistance in the area ....

When the American Allies had reached the Piazza at the top of Monteforte, a GI from New Jersey had spied an American calendar, hanging in the *"Bar Salerno"*, with the name of a local haberdasher he knew back home, and inquired of the proprietor: who had given it to him?

He was told the story of a Giuseppe Sartoriani, a local son of Monteforte Cilento, who had eloped with his beloved Carmela just after the last war to seek his fortunes with his beautiful, young bride in the New Country.

Carmela was a descendant of the local brigand-heroes, *I Fratelli Capozzoli*.

Both Giuseppe Sartoriani's and Carmela Capozzoli's families had been dead-set against the union, but their love was stronger than the ancient bonds and feuds of blood and, thus, Pèppo and Carmela had absconded with each other to leave this heavy, suffocating ballast behind them.

The young couple went together, illicitly to the Land of Boundless Opportunity, where one's past was less important than what one made of one's future.

There, Giuseppe Sartoriani had set up a simple, but professional tailor shop, which would soon be making, selling, altering, dry-cleaning the attire of the rich and famous in the little-sister Garden State of the great Empire State of New York.

The lads stayed far and away from the Bar area as that was where they had encountered the rapacious "*Lupo*" the previous October, and American troops were still stationed there to protect the town from any potentially remaining, secreted Axis forces.

****

Now it is time for the lads' beloved bedtime routine: Nonna Domenica's stories!

Tonight, she tells them one of their very favorite accounts: the story of *"u Munaciedd'"* -- *il Monaciello* -- the impish little mischievous Monk-man of the weefolk.

Like a red-capped, capricious trollet, dwarf, or gnome, he willfully causes problems and mischief.

Some say he was brought to these parts almost a thousand years ago, from the ancient lands and legends of the Scandinavians, when descendants of the Northmen ruled their southern Italian Kingdom of Sicily, having gotten stuck there on their way to the Crusades in Holy Jerusalem, while helping a local ruler.

Other legends have him living in the damp, murky underground canals and passageways of Naples, a deformed, forsaken offspring of a forbidden, cursed love.

Yet others say he was spit out from a cavern's mouth whose secret, hidden chambers linked directly to the deepest inner circles of Hell's Inferno itself.

Whatever his origins, his existence and magical abilities were not questioned in these parts.

As if to underscore this, the lads hear something metallic dropping in the animals' stalls and the braying of a donkey.

Giuseppe grabs onto his older cousin, who wriggles himself out of the little boy's hold, pretending to have no fear, goose-bumps arriving and at attention on his skin, nevertheless.

Nonna crosses herself – the boys following suit -- and begins with the story.

" *Zi Eliu e u Munaciedd'* "

*Down in Paestum, your Nonno's brother Elio was
working on the farm where their uncle Pietro raised the
lugubrious, plodding, horned water buffalo that amazingly
produced an angelic-white, ambrosial mozzarella.*

*One day, as a young man of about 14 or 15, in late
summer as Autumn was approaching, your Zio Elio was
resting after his siesta of hard salami, dark bread, goat
cheese, and wine and taking his "pisolino" -- to recover from
working in the artichoke and tomato fields and tending those
ponderous, lumbering, hooved beasts, now still out in the
fields under the olive trees, before he would take them in later
in the evening, ... when a small stone almost imperceptibly
struck him on the chest, as he was lying down, half-asleep,
enjoying the shade, under a massive bark-shedding
eucalyptus.*

At first he thought it was an insect vexing and bedeviling him, so swept he did, reflexively, absentmindedly across his chest, and dozed off again after additionally swiping blindly across his face, eyes still closed in languor ...but it repeated itself, and this time a small stone struck his face below his cheek on his right stubbly jaw.

Propping himself up, now peevish from being disturbed, he looked around and fleetingly spotted something red, -- something that looked like a small boy with a red cap -- above the animals' stall, through a smallish window, behind which hay would be put for storage for the winter, in the top storey.

Zio Elio turned his sight back to the red he had seen and squints to focus on the diminutive apparition materializing in the window...his heart begins to pick up pace as he realizes it might be "u Munaciedd' "!

Approaching the stall, he now clearly saw that the wee homunculus was gesturing to him from above, motioning to him, half-hidden, impishly, around an old beam-frame.

Now moving more quickly, waking fully from his drowsiness, Elio took a ladder... knowing that the Munacielli, if you can befriend them, will lead you to hidden ancient treasures...,

...and he went gingerly, but cautiously up the rungs.

Once young Elio was just below the window – which not even a grown child could climb through –, the Monk-man motioned to his mouth in the universally-understood sign of "hunger".

Understanding the desire of the little imp, Elio went up one more rung and turned slightly around at the precarious head of the ladder, tapping his right shoulder, whereupon the weight of the Monaciello settled onto his back, having understood the teenager's welcoming assistance, small arms and clawey fingers holding on tightly and securely around the young man's neck.

Safely down the ladder, Elio brought his precious attainment to the spot under the tree where he had had his repast, there squatting down onto his haunches to let the imp descend unharmed.

Elio looked around to make sure that none of his relatives, friends, or paesani were nearby...his sense of possession and impending riches whetting his greed.

Together they settled under the serpent-skin-shedding bark of the eucalyptus, near the rough-linen lunch sack with Elio's unfinished salami and cheese morsels; there was still even a not-too-tiny swiglet of sweet homemade wine left in the dark brown ceramic bottle.

Elio watched in fascination and wonder as the small man enjoyed the meagre but tasty vittles with a Dionysian gusto.

Like a hungry friar, the diminutive monk-man even smacked his lips and wiped them with the right sleeve of his heavy, dark frock.

They played together a simple game of rough-hewn stone marbles, until the wizened little man stood up from his crouch and motioned with his little index figure back to the hole above the ladder, leaning against the stall.

Then, as if remembering his gentlemanly duties and the rules of gratefulness established from time immemorial, as a token of appreciation for Elio's hospitality and generosity, the Monaciello reached into the folds of his vestments and brought forth a small, ancient, ancient glistening gold coin, proffering it daintily, lightly smiling, to their Great Uncle Elio.

*No words passed between the two beings in all this time;
Elio nodded in thanks, briefly but sincerely.*

*Elio lowered himself onto his haunches and turned his
back so that his little "friend" could once again climb onto
his massive shoulders for the ride back up home.*

******

[All through Nonna's story, the boys sat on their
linen-covered straw bed, transfixed, eyes widened as
if to capture by sight every word she said, their
diminutive espresso demi-tasses safely on a simple
night stool to the side.
Nonna paused to sip from her own espresso…
and then continued….]

******

*The by-now-familiar weight of this strange burden, of the
Monaciello on his back as he remounted the ladder, brought
back to his mind tales and tips from Elio's own Bisnonna:*

-- If you are able to seize the Monaciello's pointed red cap, the little monk-man will be forced to give you anything you wish to get it back! Including all of his hidden treasures of gold and precious jewels!

Elio's heart and breath missed a beat on a step as he climbed up, causing the little friar onus to also tighten up... did he sense something? Were they clairvoyant?

The teenager and his diminutive ward finally came once again to the small opening to the hay store. Outwardly, all seemed calm and normal demeanor.

Inside Elio, however, his curiosity and greed had crescendoed and finally overwhelmed the better of him:

As the Munaciedd' turned to go back to the far reaches of the stacked hay, Elio shot out his right hand and arm to take away the pointed sacred little red cap that protects the Munaciedd's bald pate.

HE WAS SUCCESSFUL!!!

Elio Salerno held the red felt hat in his own hand, free of its owner.

With this strong-arm, extortive method, power was his!

He could now get hold of the awaiting heaping mounds of golden, glistening wealth!

And then, in that brief fractional splintered moment of unconcentration, all that the powerful youth sensed was an unexpected, surprising ringing in his left ear, spreading to his upper jaw, his cheek, his face;

...followed by subsequent sensations of pain, spinning dizziness, the light of his vision fading in a rapidly diminishing circle of blackness rimmed by sparkle-stars.

His legs became lost to his conscious control; his arms left their securing hold; gravity pulled him uncontrolledly back and down and down and....

******

[The two boys sucked in
and held their breaths....]

******

SPLOTCH

Elio landed softly, albeit ignominiously, into a cushioning, mephitic pile of mud and manure!

****

[The boys break out into gleeful, uncontrolled laughter, imagining their great uncle covered in mud and stinky manure!

((The whole family, in fact the whole village of Paestum by the Sea, and now even up here in the Mountains of the Cilento, knew that Zio Elio was notoriously famous for always looking for an easy, lazy, quick win, and even now, in his advanced age, he would get himself into embarrassing predicaments.

For example, there was the time, quite recently, actually, when someone sold him a chicken that was claimed to lay double the number of eggs of a normal chicken.

In fact, the hen turned out to be too old to even lay any more eggs at all!

The trickster had swapped some additional eggs under her by some shady legerdemain to attest to her egg-laying prowess. Luckily, she could be used for a soup, but Elio had been scalped of more lire than the tough, chewy meat was worth.))

Relieved, too, the lads were that the tension had been broken.

Nonna's heart overflows with endearing joy at the innocence and pleasure of her grandsons' laughing.

She brings the story to its conclusion....]

****

Thereafter, the Munaciello climbed down the rungs of the ladder, agilely, assured, simian-fast.

Self-composed, regally, he stood above his oppressor, who was now gradually coming back to consciousness, waking while wallowing, coming to the realization of his predicament.

The Monk-man held his arms reprovingly akimbo, locating mentally what he was looking for – then, quickly, with his delicate, nimble fingers, he reached into the dazed, greedy teenager's unbuttoned shirt pocket, snatched up and out a soft cigarette packet there, at the same time turning it over and shaking out the gleaming Persian daric coin that he had gifted just moments before as a sign of goodwill.

He did not need to recover his cherished red cap, as he had already taken it swiftly and gracefully back into possession simultaneously when he had smacked Elio on the left side of his face. It sat securely, where it belonged, on the Munaciello's head.

Dazedly raising his head and upper body up onto his elbows in the dark green-brown oozey goo, Elio saw a red cap flash as it disappeared back into the pineta, never to be seen again

— absconded into a parallel realm together with his gold coin, his masculine pride, and Elio's remaining delicious salami in his rough linen food sack.

****

Nonna's eyes twinkle mischievously, lovingly, and have grown wide and even greener.

Nonetheless, she adds, saying semi-sternly,

"Stay away from the Munaciello, my boys!

If he follows you home and gets into our house or our stalls, he will break dishes and cause the animals' milk to run dry and cause you to hit your heads or elbows or stub your toes!

In the night he will nip at your toes and fingers and steal your blankets! He will only cause you trouble and woe!"

Nonna crosses herself, which makes the children's hair stand on end. Giuseppe needs to go to the bathroom soon…

"Nonna," inquires Giuseppe after a moment of consideration, *"does the father of the Munaciedd' live on Monte Chianiello?"*

Nonna Domenica caught her breath midway, and her eyes narrowed slightly,

"Why do you ask, Peppino?"

Pasqualino squeezed his cousin's hand under the blankets of their straw bed, in the unspoken gesture between the two of them that the little one should be cautious of what he was saying.

Pèppe looks at his older cousin, and then back to Nonna,

"Because there is a dark forest after the brooklet, Nonna, and that would be a good place for the Munaciedd' and his family to live."

Nonna, considered this, taking it deep into her soul, into the recesses and archives of, to them, her ancient memory, and the lines of her face smoothened in what the children would have recognized as wistfulness, had they been older.

"Yes, Giuseppe, you are right. And the woods are dark and deep in places, with wild animals and other mysterious creatures lurking about —

... ready to snatch up small, disobedient children.

Perhaps that is, indeed, where the Munaciedd' lives when he comes to Monteforte — or perhaps one of his siblings or cousins is there.

So you and Lino be sure to stay on the path and don't move too far away from the goats and the clearing, my dear-hearts."

Nonna, had the wisdom of years and of raising almost a dozen children and knew the psychology of not totally forbidding things to the children, lest this result in the very opposite of her intentions.

"Yes, my Nonna," Pèppe nodded vigorously, his beautiful red locks jiggling as curlied, spring-wound hair does when the head to which it belongs moves quickly.

The little one gets up and excuses himself to use their outside latrine.

Domenica would have to tell her daughter Filomena to cut this little boy's red locks soon, before the high summer arrived bringing with it dangerous infestations of lice and fleas.

She didn't want to have to shave him completely bald and dust his little pate with the DDT powder the Allied soldiers had brought with them.

"Of course, Nonna," adjoined Pasqualino.

"We will keep watch over the goats and be careful!"

Nonna, nodded in agreement, but knew, too, of Pasqualino's wily deceptiveness and craftiness ….

****

As was the comforting, repeated flow of their bedtime routine, she spoke some prayers and incantations over them once little Giuseppe had returned, crossing herself with them in unison.

The boys are tucked under their blankets, and she gathers their empty *tazzine.*

Then kissing both of them lovingly, she moved to her own straw bed-cot in the cooking-living area, to await Francesco's return from the *Bar Salerno.*

****

Giuseppe dreams of bees and honey hives --
gigantic bees that take him, the goats, and Lisetta
away to an enormous hive ruled by a golden-
crowned queen who held a ruby-red pomegranate.

Her minions are brown-frocked dwarves with
scarlet caps and glistening green eyes.

During the night, Lino is awakened by a slight
whistling-wind in his ear and the small hairs on his
neck stand on end.

His rational mind gradually gathers back strength,
and he turns around to find little Giuseppe close to
his head, on his very pillow, breathing gently,
somewhat wheezingly.

Pasqualino, now calmed and reassured that
neither the little Monk-man, nor any of the other
occupants of the Campanian night, has entered
their chambers to teasingly plague them, covers
himself and falls back into a fitful sleep.

In Pasqualino's dreams, the Giambone and the
Munaciedd' start mixing and melding into one in his
subconscious, sleeping mind….

In the morning, the boys' woolen coverlet is lying on the floor....

CHAPTER 10

The Sunday tradition was mass at around 8:30 – give-or-take a few minutes, at the Chiesa di Santa Maria Assunta…lots of incense, tinkling of bells, timed, choreographed standing, sitting, kneeling, sitting, praying, reciting, standing, kneeling, ….

The ornate statue of Monteforte's Patron Saint, San Donato, was in the church at this time, having been brought up from his chapel further down Monte Chianiello in the annual procession on the 20th of May.

Festivals, food, and family always followed the somber, sacred ceremonies.

Good-natured, but Methuselah-yeared Padre Massimiliano falls asleep when one of the Church elders reads ploddingly slow from the Gospels …

...a young acolyte, familiar with the padre's weaknesses needs to nudge him back awake for the liturgies of the remainder of the service.

During the message to the congregation, the aging *Sacerdote* tells his flock of the long-hoped-for, momentous news that their Rome, the Eternal City whose mere name causes a swell of pride in every Italian's heart, whether they be *Polentone* or *Terrone,* has been liberated.

Roma é libera!

A murmur went up as they learned that Italy's ancient capital had finally been liberated from the Teutonic madness their King and his anointed Duce had brought down upon them.

But the Duce was still active and spitting venom from his puppet *Repubblica Sociale Italiana di Salò* up in the North, bordering German-annexed Austria.

The conflagration was not over yet.

Just during the previous weeks, in early May, a destroyed Monte Cassino had been taken over by the Allied Forces, but only after the Pope had given permission to bomb and rout the in-nested Northern Forces from this sacred, ancient abbey and monastery, originally founded by St. Benedict himself.

The battles had cost many, many lives, some unnecessarily....

Padre Massimiliano led them in a prayer for the souls of the lost – both military and civilian. This had become a heart-rending part of their Sunday services for the past too many years, indeed decades.

Not infrequently one of the female congregants, sometimes with their children, would break out into tears and sobbing.

Others simply sat staring up emptily, pitifully at the Cross above the altar, their heads and faces covered in black-laced veils, a tear streaming down after a spasm of remembrance distorts their face and they look down into their laps.

Only women and children were in the Church itself for the entire service – many nonnas and also younger women whose men had been killed in fighting were wearing the black of mourning and *lutto*. It was usual for widows to wear black for the remainder of their lives....

The old men and those of the able-bodied others who had not been conscripted or otherwise involved in yet another European conflict, stood just outside of the church, near the entrance... sometimes smoking, silent and somber, grinding and grinding the tiny remaining butts strenuously, forcefully, bitterly under their worn shoes on the steps leading up into the church ... until the last tiny ember of light and fire was extinguished.

Giuseppe's Mother – Filomena -- Teresa's sister, and the Rossi children were there, too.

This was a traditional duty all of them fulfilled before they were released back to taking care of their goat and sheep herds for a shortened day of grazing.

Though sometimes ambivalent toward the Church and its demands – especially by the male inhabitants, habit, superstition, and social interest made it a central element of their births, lives, and deaths.

Mamma kissed her mother, her sister, and the boys, and left just after the service to make her way once again to Magliano, this time with no burdening onus upon her other than love and sociability.

She and her sister-in-law would have much to share that late-morning and afternoon…..

Teresa had dark rings under her eyes and looked ashen and thin. Domenica knew the cause, but was concerned, nevertheless: for many days now her daughter had been tormented by a painful drumming in her temples and at the lower back of her head.

Nunzio was still safe as far as she knew. With the Canadian and American troops. But who truly knew? except the Fates, who hold the threads of our lives in their pitiless hands…and for how long?

****

Padre Massimiliano now concludes the liturgy as
it had been done for centuries upon centuries:

"In nomine Patris, et Filii, et Spiritus Sancti. Amen."
making the sign of the Cross over his flock.

The two boys rush out and away, their Nonna
knowing they had responsibilities to take care of
with their sustaining, constantly hungry animals.

Mamma had made her departures and had already
left the church.

Nonna had catching-up to do with her circle of
relatives, *cumare,* friends, but this did not lessen her
duties toward her grandsons.

*"Don't forget to change your clothes and take your sacks
with the merendine!"*

… Nonna calls after them in admonishing
reminder, to their backs as they weave amongst,
in, and out of the clustered groups of women and
children of the congregation, away down the central
aisle of Santa Maria Assunta.

"Sì, Nonna!" answers Pèppe over his shoulder.

"Sapime, Nô!" – *"We know, Nonna!"*
was Pasqualino's response.

"And be back for pranzo," she added sternly.

Pasqualino simply nodded silently in agreement
to this last admonition as he continued away with
his cousin.

Quickly upon reaching home, Pasqualino and
Giuseppe take off their Sunday best – not more
than simply less-used, washed twins of their more
worn-in daily work clothes;

…their shoes were the same but had been
blackened and softened for Sunday Mass with black
ash and a touch of swine lard.

The day was beautiful and warm, redolent of the
maturing plants and grasses, early June bringing
with it the deeper, less-intense, quieter aromas past
spring yet before the parching dryness of high
summer.

The lads would be cautious that day because they did not know exactly when Mamma would be returning from her Sunday visit to her brother Luigi's and her sister-in-law Elena's.

Teresa enjoyed being with her beloved brother, his wife Elena, and their 2 little girls –
Anna, the eldest at 4, and Irene, 2.

The sisters-in-law always chattered excitedly when sharing cooking and household secrets and the latest news with each other.

Teresa Acquaviva took delight in these times, especially in the moments with her two dear young nieces.

She also felt relieved and lighter after their time together, the burdens of her responsibilities lifted for a few salubrious, restorative hours…. they gave her energy to face yet another new week without her husband.

******

Lisetta and the goats are mustered and herded friskily and efficiently, the boys behind them, Pèppe seated proudly and Pascha-like upon his noble mount, Pasqualino pulling on the leather tether.

They could have been on their way to Bethlehem.

The weather was behaving nicely at their pasture, and the goats flowed down from the path onto the slightly lower-down pasture, like a living wave of earth-toned hair and horns, onto a shore of green and yellows and pinks and minute blues.

Mamma had gone directly from the Mass onto the path she was so familiar with and was already almost in Magliano by the time the boys were at their pasture.

Lino knew they had only about two or, at most, three hours of secure, safe time to go a few hundred meters further along the mysterious trail they had discovered the previous day.

Again, they waited for the Rossi herd to come along...

… Pèppe's older siblings having lingered in the Church a bit longer than the young'uns, to enjoy the presence of the other male and female teenagers they knew....but when Lino saw them approaching, and the twins already taunting and catcalling them from a small distance away, he demonstrably grabbed Pèppe and skedaddled with him to a low rock at the farthest end of the pasture…

…knowingly letting himself be seen, to fix firmly into the older Rossis' perceptions that the boys were more or less anchored safely, soundly, securely in their duties with the goats.

Domenico and Francesca run a few meters toward them, but stop and lose interest in the pursuit, swiping away backwards and downwards, disparagingly in the air with their palms facing the earth, as they turned to return to their herds – giving to understand that the boys were not worth the trouble to chase after today…especially since their minds and hearts were still filled with memories of their encounters with peers of the opposite sex.

****

"I'm so glad they didn't grab and tickle me again, Lino",
states little Giuseppe as he hands Michele's gloves
up to Giuseppe, putting the finishing touches on
their daunting, minatory Archangel.

Today, their "guardian" is at another location of
the pasture.

*"Yes, Pèppe. Those twins think they are so tough and
strong. Just wait until we grow up…we'll show them!"*
Lino states emphatically, strengthening the two
younger ones' alliance in their smallness.

Preparing for their expedition, strengthening
themselves for the exertions of their upcoming
adventurous foray into the forest, the lads nibble
down a portion of the hard cheese, hard bread – the
viscuotti, almost stone-hard salami Nonna had
prepared and packed away for them, and take a few
swallows of their water.

They then set off….

****

"Hmmm, managia! Where the devil is it?

Why did we leave Lisetta down at the pasture?"

… imprecated Lino, searching for the beginning of the secret path, but not finding it immediately, attempting curses of not quite the order of magnitude the adults could let out.

This time, they had left Lisetta to stay with the herd, since they expected to be adventuring a bit longer this Sunday and wanted to be nimble, flink, and fast.

"Here it is, Lino," indicated his smaller, closer-to-the-ground cousin, drawing back gingerly a small thorny shrub to reveal trampled, flattened earth.

How well the way was concealed!

Even at Pasqualino's slightly more generally advantageous height, the shrubbery, the primulae, and other wildflowers, grasses cloaked well the secret trail leading up the slope of the mountain. It was actually easier to see when one was closer to the ground – like Giuseppe!

As they retraced their steps gradually upwards, after fording again the small brook whose water is diminishing daily with the thirsty, encroaching summer, the familiar droppings re-appeared, accompanied by their coterie of zaftig, bristled flies and lesser entomological varieties – the myrmidons of manure.

They pass, too, one-after-the-other, the now familiar *"nuraghette"*, the "hives" they had discovered on their first excursion into this hidden realm.

The boys continue on and up, seeing several more of the peculiar, some slightly flattened, domed structures: -- three, four, five, …

…how many more were there? … each one containing something different:

… a simple suet candle, a pink or crystal-white quartz stone, a fossilized ammonite, a clay-sculpted image of a fantastical creature that they did not recognize;

… each one covered, camouflaged in a different manner.

They follow the invisible direction the empty, open eyes of the nuraghette point them in.

Lulled now into a false sense of security due to the constantly disappointed expectation of encountering an actual beehive skep, Giuseppe incautiously reaches into the hole at the base of one of these odd little domes with his left hand…

…and withdraws it almost immediately …

screaming!

It was actually a woven bee-skep!!!

"Pèppe! What's the matter???!!!"

implores Pasqualino urgently, caringly apprehensive.

"A bee, a BEE!!!"

agonized out little Giuseppe, his face grimacing with pain – alternatingly holding his now red, swelling left hand with his right, shaking it, crying out, circling about in a wild uncontrolled jig!

"Ow! Ow! It hurts so MUCH, Lino!"

"Help me! Help me!"

Pasqualino tried to hold his little cousin, to comfort him, but he kept breaking away, jumping to try to ease his pain and distress.

Pasqualino Acquaviva was starting to feel panic now – what if….?

Little did the children know, let alone hear, that above Pèppe's excruciating cries, about 100 meters further up the mountain side, a large beige-white hound had begun a deep, bass barking.

Reacting suddenly, intuitively, and swiftly passing the barking dog, came the now uncloaked Giambone, dropping, as he moved, a hoe he had just been using for whatever uncanny things he did up there.

Again, he appeared suddenly at the boys' side, as he had on the previous occasion, but now without his heavy coat, only in a sleeveless sheep's wool undershirt under his leather suspenders,

… sweating with an old, animal-human stank.

A red bandana was tied around his neck to keep him safe from cold drafts.

Arriving at the tormented child's side, he knelt down, quickly and nimbly for his age, his large rough hands taking hold of the agitated Pèppe and calming him with incomprehensible, soothing words of an Italian they did not recognize.

Mesmerized, but still agitated, sniffing and red, wet-faced, the little child calmed enough for the old man to gently take the swollen pawlet into his massive hand.

Giuseppe's little fingers had become the size of one of Nonno Francesco's salumetti, albeit one of the littler ones.

From one of his pockets, Giambone took out a thin, supple, soft-leather pouch, which seemed to contain unctuous-looking little strips of black and brown hair snippings from a wild black boar.

A wafting smell of tobacco reaches Giuseppe's nostrils, remind him of his father and his cigarettes, distract him for an instant from his suffering.

A fraction later, Pasqualino smells it, too.

One hand holding Giuseppe's bitten one, the other holding the pouch, the mysterious elder tells Pasqualino in a calm, firm, authoritative but not frightening voice to take out a small pinch of the boar hairs, put them into the palm of his hand, moisten it with some of his spittle, and then knead it gently, being careful not to lose any of it.

Pasqualino Acquaviva follows the old man's instructions correctly, exactly.

Having finished the preparation, the Giambone takes the dampened wad from Lino's upturned palm, squeezes out some of the brown liquid, and rubs it gently onto the little reddening Vesuvius on the back of Pèppe's hand, onto the small pinpoint that is the summit of the volcano.

Bunching the wad up together, he removes the insect's stinger that had still been injecting poison into the little boy's bloodstream, even after it had been eviscerated from the honeybee worker in this last act of ultimate sacrifice for her hive.

The little lad had been fortunate that he had not disturbed, riled up more of the diligent laborers of the colony.

The attacking bee herself succumbed to its last throes, giving up her diminutive but lion-hearted ghost somewhere on the earth around the base of the hive.

The Giambone then sucks out some of the poison from Giuseppe's hand and spits it away into the underbrush.

"Once more,"

directs Giambone to Lino, now obediently following the procedure they had just gone through.

The ancient man puts this second nicotined wad onto Giuseppe's hand, pressing it down, simultaneously standing up and heading back down the hill, down the path, toward the normal route from the villages of the Cilento through the forest, leading little Giuseppe tenderly with him.

Pasqualino now simply trots silently, respectfully behind them, looking very much the little boy he actually still is – an amiable, large, beige-white dog at his side now – wondering what was to become of the cousin he loved so dearly, though never daring to admit it out loud....

CHAPTER 11

Pasqualino needn't have worried.

Once at the small ford of the Alento's tribulet, Giambone washes Giuseppe's hand in the cold mountain water...the pain and swelling already abating due to the effects of the tobacco wad-pack.

After several cleansing ablutions, Giuseppe is no longer whimpering as he realizes that his little chubby paw is recovering.

As a final unguent, Giambone takes some fresh mud from the bank of the stream and makes a compress with a clean but greying linen handkerchief he had taken from his back pocket, that he always has with him, at the ready, out of professional habit.

"You owe me quite a lot, little one!" he says gruffly, but with twinkling eyes, to the curly red-mopped boy with green eyes he knew too well....

"Sí, Signore. Sí...Grazie..." Giuseppe lowers his eyes, almost ashamed.

His happiness is regained when the large dog comes up behind him and tickling licks his right ear!

Lino has now come over, too, to pet the friendly animal's large furry white head, who is now smiling in that obvious canine joy that proves that dogs have souls, panting and tongue lolling from the side.

"So, you've made friends with Mimma, I see!
But get back to your goats now...
I'm sure you've told your mother where you are...
Right?"

"Yes, of course Sir — Mamma knows we are up here,"

...Pasqualino prevaricated after a moment of consideration....

"Hmmm…I see…." the Giambone looked down from one child to the other, unconvinced, as the two stared up at him, wide-eyed to give credence to their fibbing.

"Go now and be careful. Keep putting fresh mud on the little Red-Head's bite and wash it off in fresh spring water," he prescribed, looking closely at Giuseppe's hand, *"It looks like he is going to survive this one."*

As the boys and the old man are about to separate, a thought enters the Giambone's mind:

"And come back in two Sundays then, if you want, at the same time as now, so that I can inspect the bite to see if everything is healed properly.
I will have finished with the hoeing and planting preparations by then."

And then almost as an afterthought,

"Would you like to learn about those little hives? Those pesky little creatures who buzz around and live in them aren't as nasty as they appeared to the two of you today. They make some delicious honey, too!"

"Oh yes, yes!" agree the lads enthusiastically ... and he shook hands with them to seal their agreement, as men do.

"My greetings to your parents…and your grandparents."

Jumping daintily over the little ford area of the rivulet, the boys ran down the path to their home pasture.

******

Unluckily, Mamma returned from her brother's and sister-in-law's in Magliano Vetere a bit earlier that particular day, but luckily for Lino and Pèppe -- perhaps due to the intervening "fortuitous" event of the bee-bite that had cut their meanderings in the Giambone's realm short --, just soon after the boys had returned to their pasture, quickly dismantled and hidden Michele, and had once again settled in with their flocks after the stinging beehive incident.

Pèppe had already begun again to collect some wildflowers and dandelions, as their beauty and fragrance distracted and delighted him _and_ drew the goats to him for some playful feeding with these delectable forest friands.

Lisetta lies placidly and content under the shade of a chestnut, resting and munching some grass.

Teresa Salerno Acquaviva, Pasqualino's mother, Giuseppe's aunt, is carrying back with her on her head a light, medium-sized, wicker-woven basket containing the gifts of kindling fatwood, interspersed with some bread, viscuotti, and hard salami "unexpectedly" yet predictably received from her sister-in-law and her brother.

She hands the two lads some confetti, and fennel- and almond-stuffed dried figs from her stay, from her simple dress pocket, continuing to balance the much-lighter-than-usual but especially cherished load upon her head.

Talks to them briefly she does and looks at them carefully, and...

… something seems awry in their behavior once again, but she cannot determine what it is:

Pasqualino is avoiding looking at her directly or glances only briefly, moving from foot to foot as if unsettled by something, preoccupied;

Giuseppe keeping his hands almost unnaturally behind his back....

"Pasqualino," she begins with that special tone only a mother can do, that with its very sound pierces the inner recesses of one's soul, *"what have you two been...."*

Before she can complete her words, little Pèppe brings forth his hands from behind him:

A darling bouquet of delicate small mountain flowers – bright yellow, fluorescent purple-pink, blue, white, red – in his small left paw, covering his hand over like a floral glove!

Zia Teresa's eyes are drawn to it, widening, the young woman moved by its beauty and intricate delicateness...

… perhaps also because her soul and spirit are more relaxed that afternoon from the healing, liberating blessings of her visit in Magliano Vetere.

Bending down with straight hips, neck, and back, almost as if curtsying, the load still balanced above her, she takes the *mazzolino di fiori,* the mountain nosegay, with her left hand from his.

"Grazie, Pèppe! Com'é bello!" she thanks her little nephew, as he steps back, returning his little hands behind him in what she interprets is respect and politeness as he fixes his eyes on her face, taking in the smiling joy coming from hers.

After taking in the floral delight of its fragrance, Teresa puts the little posy blindly, yet gently, up onto a safe spot of her burden, only by touch, feeling an additional time to make sure it was safe and sound.

She gingerly tossles her nephew's red curls as a sign of gratefulness.

Mamma is completely lulled into a feeling of safety; only tenuous, negligible wisps of cautious suspicion remaining.

Finally reassured and somewhat under time pressure to help her Mother with the late-afternoon meal preparations, Teresa continues on down to her home village of Monteforte Cilento, smiling back at the boys.

"Don't be late for pranzo, Pasqualí!"

she reminds them.

The two cousins stood together watching as she disappeared down the path before they relaxed, their tenseness released.

Giuseppe was once again holding and gently caressing, now freely in front of him, his still swollen left hand in his right.

It was still tender and warm but visibly becoming better.

He ran quickly the short distance back to the stream to cool it down even further and for some fresh mud to make a soothing pack.

Too, Pasqualino realized now that he and little Giuseppe must be particularly cautious when they return to the Giambone again in the coming weeks.

Frank A. Merola

CHAPTER 12:
La Grotta del Giambone – Giambone's Cave

The agreed-upon two Sundays had passed, with the boys' interest and excitement increasing, growing, and piqued.

The people of this area were used to folks of all ages being scraped and cut and sometimes bones broken – or worse -- because of the hardness of life here in the South and especially here on the mountain, so Giuseppe's now diminished bee-sting, a mere blackened point, raised absolutely no notice, not at this point in its healing.

Which was just as well....

Their Mothers had never seen the boys so assiduous and careful in carrying out their duties.

They were pleased to see that they were developing into responsible youngsters, especially now that so many of the village's men were away...or worse.

Lino and Pèppe have become, through several times of practice, more efficient in their preparation of their diversionary, precautionary tactic of the Arcangelo Michele.

On this second Sunday, they have retraced their steps up the secret path toward the beehive, this time treating it with the due respect...

...Giuseppe hiding his little hands under his armpits as they make a wide safe circle around the individual bees swarming slowly, lazily in the noonday sunlight.

It is now after the middle of June and the ground under the forest canopy is still damp from a brief, light rain the evening before, but the air is warm and clear as the sun's rays pierce through the trees that make up the forest's protective cover of foliage.

The water in the rivulet has lessened even more, and fording it requires little effort, other than the requisite caution to not stumble over an unstable stone or slip off of a mossy rock.

As they come closer and closer to the place where they had last been, Lino spies two further nuraghette and the path linking them, continuing, again, up and beyond them.

He becomes conscious, once again, that any opening in the little flattened-domed structures face in the direction of the next "milestone".

Too, some of these hive-like structures are truly round-domed, without a flattened top.

Thus, the cousins rise further up the slope...until Mimma appears from behind some bushes and begins barking joyfully at them.

The boys no longer hear warning aggression in her bark, but rather a welcoming, "Come on up! Come on up!" in her voice.

Fear has left the boys, but a cautious respect remains in the older lad.

Giuseppe begins running up to her as she then dives into the underbrush to reduce the distance separating them and meet him half-way, as it were.

She breaks out from some ground-hugging leafy plants right in front of Giuseppe

The joy of children with loving animals is exuberated here in this idyllic sylvan moment when the chubby red-head and the beige-white dog meet once again.

Giambone appears some 30 meters higher up, at the place where Mimma had come into view, and he calls them to come up to him, to continue following the path, well-disguised, but apparent once it has been navigated.

The happy band of boys and beast finally reach the lookout point where Mimma had stood, her eyrie from where she could observe any and all approaching up the hidden pathway.

Surprised when they reach the spot, they had expected here to encounter the sheer wall of a flank of Monte Chianiello.

But where they stood was not a wall of their Mother Mountain at all, but a natural ridge about four or five meters wide, a ridge-back, a geological backbone, grassy, wild-flowered, and riddled here and there by large stones, behind which the land fell in a gentler slope than the one they had come up.

And this falling land behind and beyond the ridge now became, exposed to them, a secretive ravine valley.

Yet, from below, this small ravine, this protected "glen" was completely hidden from view, invisible…one would believe that the mountain's wall simply continued up unbroken -- until one was actually on the ridge they were standing on, and saw that it contained large clearings and small pastures.

Giambone's secret pastures were a hidden natural sanctuary, an enclosed, almost alpine swath in a breach in the imposing body of Monte Chianiello.

Hornbeam hardwood trees, as well as maple, flowering ash, and oak, and chestnuts populate the edges of this area and all through its swath.

Large and small patches of boulders, slowly becoming overgrown with grasses and shrubs, are like the squat menhirs of giants, dropped here and there.

No one from the village had ever talked about this place, as far as the boys were aware.

Later they would learn that it had been cultivated by Giambone's skills and it was fertile and productive.

As they followed along this backbone, to the left down in the small ravine, Lino and Pèppe spied a little dark, almost black, donkey, smaller than their own Lisetta and a few goats and sheep.

Straight ahead of them, along the ridgeway, almost unnoticeable because of the natural growth and bushes in front of it, stood the gaping hole of a cave, a caverna, a grotta;

… then, further up to the left of the main opening was a smaller, still largish hole, over which a small waterfall streamed, like a window opening into the hillside that wrapped, hugged around an outlier of the main mountain.

This smaller second opening was roughly almond-shaped, and the water flowing over it made it look like a sad, tearing eye.

The Giambone had covered these two rounded natural openings of the "grotta" with rough, now weather-worn planking and boards that had aged and lightly mossed over with time;

…these "doors" would not be immediately recognized or even seen, as they were set back a bit from the external mouths of these openings.

Nevertheless, the larger, main portal protected the large interior space quite snugly from the elements.

Further up the Monte Chianiello, at over 1'000 meters, was *"Lo Varco Cervone"* – a gap in the mountains where the winds from both sides, both flanks, met and swirled into each other in an aeolian embrace --

-- winds dancing together in a wild passionate whirl in this gap of the mountain on the way to the *Alburni Cervati* mountains to the North East.

Beyond this gap, down on the other side of the mountain from where the boys now stood in front of the Giambone's grotta, were fields of chestnuts and well-fed, succulent but aggressive wild pigs.

Pasqualino, Giuseppe, following behind Mimma, reach the main entrance to the cave, a cleared space covered from view by bushes and hanging ivies and flowering vines -- covered overhead, too, from the elements by an overhanging slab of slate rock from which a small rivulet, a stray from the waterfall covering the smaller window-eye came down like the single strand of a shower, further distracting attention from what lay behind it.

This was truly a place worthy of the Munaciello or at least one of his relatives!

At this summit destination, just underneath and inside of the overhanging ledge and between it and the mountain entrance to Giambone's cave, there was one final "hive", one final nuraghetta, more delicately made than the others the boys had seen.

This last one is an elegant perfect dome and has an open votive niche in which stands the sculpted figure of a woman, like the Virgin Mary, seated, holding a pomegranate in her hand, the other hand raised in blessing, but not quite Christian -- much, much older, more ancient Greek or even before.

Like the Goddess Hera....but the boys have no conception or idea of her.

Giuseppe – perceiving in the statuette the Holy Blessed Virgin -- touches her tiny clay feet with the tips of his index and middle finger of his right hand, then automatically makes the sign of the Cross – Father, Son, and Holy Spirit – then as a fourth point, makes a small chubby cross with his thumb held over his bent index finger and kisses this, too –

… a second miniature sign of the Cross within the main sign of the Cross.

Making only one Cross over oneself is not enough protection in the Campania, let alone in the Cilento….

Lino approaches the Virgin Goddess as if to pay his respects in the same manner as his more spontaneous, natural little cousin, but retracts, draws back his own hand because he does not want to seem rude and too forward at another's homestead.

In this moment, their eyes notice something beyond this shrine, further along in the shadows:

-- a large gaping entrance space reveals itself to them, their sight slowly becoming accustomed to the relative shadowy darkness after the brightness of the early afternoon, and discern that a large wooden portal, even deeper back in the stone wall of the mountain, has silently opened, and the Giambone is standing there.

He has been standing there ever since having called them up to him, had been observing their approach with Mimma and their actions at the shrine to the Goddess.

****

CHAPTER 13

Teresa's by-two-year's-younger brother Luigi and his wife, Elena Nicoletti *in Salerno* (her married name), had lived in Magliano Vetere ever since they were married.

Elena's family came from there, and they grew, harvested, and refined tobacco, olives, and were aglianico grape vintners.

The weaker, sweeter wine from the white-dusted, dark-blue skinned, light-greenish-insided *Uva Americana* was used to make a low-alcohol drink especially liked by the children.

Their fathers would even put slices of hard, sweet peaches into a glass of this latter to soak and then give them even to the teething toddlers to enjoy.

Elena, with a slightly, ever so slightly hooked nose and shiny black-bright short-cut no-nonsense hair, was almost five year's older than Luigi, and her wisdom made her seem even more dignified and mature – despite her height.

A woman very self-composed and strong of character, but of very small, but powerfully wiry, of stature.

Luigi Salerno had been spared the dangers and ravages of the war because of a bout with polio as a young child, which had left his left leg from the hip down partially paralyzed and caused him to walk with a noticeable limp.

He had been lucky – other children and adults in the area had not been and had succumbed, had suffocated to the ravages of this ancient virus.

The famed *"Drinker Pulmone di Ferro"* -- which could aid the victim's breathing while their bodies fought against this pernicious infection -- was accessible only to the wealthiest and the nobility.

An excellent hunter, nevertheless, even despite his physical infirmity, Luigi was known for his skill and acumen in bringing down especially the small deer and wild boars that roamed and snuffed and grunted in the ancient oak and chestnut forests of Monte Chianiello.
He brought down the occasional wolf, too.

Their Salerno-Nicoletti *"Salame di Cinghiale"* was known far-and-wide in this part of the Campanian Apennines and even down to the promontory fortress city of Agropoli overlooking the Tyrrhenian coast to the south of Paestum.

Luigi knew where the swine herds sought out the most succulent chestnut and acorn areas, and the randy smell of their wallowing pits – drenched and soiled in their scat and urine and feral porcine sweat -- could be scented meters away, at the base of gullies, under the safety of the roots of large trees.

One of his kneecaps bore a scar when and where, in a moment of inexcusable inattention on his part, an aggressive male in its death throes had cut through his heavy serge hunting trousers with its vicious tusks.

The boar had made an especially delectable treat that had brought them a goodly amount of lire during the Epiphany market, the *"Mercato della Befana"*, on the 6th of January a few years back.

******

Luigi's polio-induced incapacitation and its accompanying limp was the "blessing in disguise" that had kept him out of active service in the *"Esercito Italiano"* with its shifting loyalties and internal struggles.

So many had died on distant battlefields of foreign lands: in Libya, Ethiopia, Eritrea, Somalia and even on lands that had once belonged to their own Roman Empire, in the neighboring countries of France, Greece, the Balkans....

"Facetta nera" was no longer being played on the few available radios, but the catchy Fascist tune was difficult to get out of one's ears.

******

Elena was not exactly a *"Strega"* but was known for her natural intelligence, her ability to sense another's inner state and character, her wisdom, her counselling, and her knowledge of things arcane and spiritual.

People were suspicious of her powers, but always sought out her help, especially when it came to the problems that they could not understand, not admit to themselves...problems they attributed to the malignant effects of the Evil Eye.

On that Sunday, Teresa had sought out her sister-in-law's skills because of the excruciating headaches she had been having, for several weeks now... sometimes even vomiting from the agony.

Elena sensed intuitively that it was because of the absence and lack of knowledge of the state her beloved Nunzio found himself in.

After Church and the announcement of the taking of Rome -- rumors had it that the Eternal City had fallen to the Allies relatively easily because the Germans had abandoned it and escaped further North with the bulk of their troops unscathed and still *"Kampfbereit"* --

…she wondered when her husband would ever come home. It was all taking much longer than the sanguine promises of the commanding generals.

Nunzio had followed in the long Monteforte tradition of fighting for the Republic against any dictators whether internal or external – his heroes were the notorious, controversial brigands, the martyred Brothers Capozzoli.

Every day Teresa waited for news of him, repressed her concerns with work and frequent trips through the paths of Monte Chianiello through to Capizzo to Magliano Vetere and then return back to Monteforte Cilento.

The weight of the burdens on both her head and heart not to be underestimated.

Physical exertion kept her panicking fears down, suppressed them, but the weights she carried on her head in no way helped assuage or alleviate her increasingly unbearable migraines….

Elena's ceremonies did -- from the emotional release they brought, from the compassionate understanding given by another woman, together with her tears that she only revealed privately to her beloved, trusted sister-in-law.

Teresa Salerno would never show weakness in front of anyone else.

The vibrant, vital young woman couldn't recall when the headaches had begun; she had never had them until that point in her relatively short life, nor did she know that they were called migraines.

All she knew was that sometimes they pounded so mercilessly in her head, her temples, behind her eyes, that she would have to throw up, at other times writhingly, restlessly lie on the straw beds with the boys, Lino and Pèppe, playing around her or sent out to scamper around outside amongst the chickens and other creatures of the farm and fields, her responsibilities momentarily abandoned while she tried to recuperate enough to finish the myriad household chores of her days.

Medical doctors were not the first line of defense against maladies here in the South of Italy, in the hills and mountains of the Cilento, simply because there were so few of them, so few physicians, or they remained only a short time…

— one went to relatives or the made-relatives of the *cumare* and *cumpari*, or to the elderly wise women and, sometimes, but rarely, wise-men of the village.

In her desperation to combat the excruciating pains behind her eyes and temples, Teresa finally turned to Elena, whom the younger woman knew to be a believer and adept in the egregious maleficent effects of the inimical Evil Eye, the feared *"Malocchio"*.

Even in, perhaps especially in, these small villages, there were those who would become jealous of the ambition and industriousness of a vigorous, young, beautiful village compatriot with a desirable, strapping, brave young husband now fighting valiantly with and as one of their Liberators.

The young woman had always wondered why she and Nunzio had only been able to have one child so far, bright and intelligent Pasqualino, despite the healthy vigor and passion of the pair.

Teresa suspected that someone had cast, was still casting, this hexing maleficent spell on her, but she could not tell who.

There were many who desired Nunzio....

There could be no other explanation for the pain she was suffering, and thus Elena had set a date for the healing exorcism -- a Sunday afternoon, after Church, only Elena and her daughters present.

These healing powers could be passed solely onto the female progeny, from mother to daughters, and, despite her girls' young ages, Elena already wanted to test which of her two had the "gift" –

... she already suspected little two-and-a-half-year-old Irene; her by less than two-years-older sister, Anna, was already terribly vain and prissy at 4-years of life.

Teresa had fasted as a preparation and, upon Elena's instructions, both from food and from water for the previous 24 hours.

The long walk, her anticipation of healing relief and deliverance, the lack of sustenance had all made her a bit weak and woozy. Luckily, she had no heavy basket to bear today.

Knowing that it was best not to wait too much longer with the ceremony to drive away the Malocchio, Elena brought out from a special drawer the simple white porcelain dish she kept for these rites…

…and some especially virgin olive oil kept in a separate, closed tin cannister.

Luigi had been sent out of the home, gently, to see that the animals and the stalls were behaving.

Elena could have asked him to do anything: he knew his place was not with the womenfolk during the driving-out of the Evil Eye.

Too, he could simply sit away in a secluded corner of their homestead on a stump, enjoying the afternoon sun and a self-rolled scraggly cigar, under the dappled shade of a large old olive tree.

****

Sitting, more hunching over, at the top end of the oval kitchen table where Luigi's place normally was, the large round bone-white soup dish of coolish tepid-warm water inches below her nose, Teresa's eyes were closed. Only gray, indirect light imbues the dimmed room.

Elena -- dressed in black -- was standing behind the younger woman, gently rubbing Teresa's throbbing temples, reciting old incantations in Campanian, interlaced with Christian prayers in Latin;

... the little girls sat at the farther end of the table, but to the healer and afflicted's left.

Teresa's physical state did not affect her hair: long, black, waved, oiled shiny, ancient Greek, open only before other women and in cherished private night-time moments with Nunzio, flowing as if in opposition and rebellion to the bun she wore it in under her headscarf during the day.

Elena was also captivated and awed by the younger woman's beauty, charisma, aura, but had the discipline to dispel her own feelings of desire, of envy, of jealousy.

The efficacy of the elimination of the Evil Eye would be rendered useless, impotent, if the "sorceress" did not empty her own vessel of this ancient, destructive, all-too-mighty monster.

From the combined stresses on her body of a migraine, a lack of food and fluids, the long walk to Magliano Vetere, Elena's ritual was timed for just this moment:

Teresa was near the point of collapse and losing a grasp on the reality around her, the tension in her body, her neck, her shoulders slowly spontaneously already gradually loosening with the chanting and massaging.

She lifts her eyes to the Cross hanging on the wall behind and above the girl-children's heads, above the new portrait of Marshall Badoglio of the Kingdom of Italy, the loving but firm, rhythmically massaging fingers of Elena's hands putting her into a light trance in which the pain is slowly assuaged, begins to dissipate from her body.

"Calm yourself, my sister – Calmati, sogre'me,"
Elena intones hypnotically.

The two toddler-girls are there on the other side of the table, but only little Irene has become transfixed with a concerned, concentrated interest on her aunt and on her mother;

Anna begins losing attention, is becoming impatient, nervous, and squirms to get down off her chair and goes off to play with her ragdoll in a corner of the cooking area, near the rough-hewn stone fireplace.

Teresa finds concentrating on the little girls and their movements increasingly difficult and then her vision blurs.

Irene in her simple, faded-gray gingham Sunday frock and tousle-top of brown curls pinned down on one side with a shiny filigreed butterfly clasp (brought back from Germany by a male relative who had been conscripted by the Nazis to build grenades and other munitions in Berlin) seems to transform, to Teresa's perception, into a golden-crowned homunculus – an elven creature who climbs onto the table and dances thereon in slow voodoo rhythms;

… a red skullcap in the middle of the crown radiates between its crenellations…the monarch monklet's liquid-green emerald eyes and puckered mouth mocking her…

… casting names and suspicions of who amongst her circle could be casting the Evil Eye on her, trying to destroy her dreams, her beloved, her entire young life….

Without breaking the rhythm of the temple massaging, in a calm clear gentle yet authoritative tone, Elena tells her silent sister-in-law, conviction and power in her own words,

*"Someone is trying to harm you, my blessed sister,
my little dear one...*

Why? Jealousy. And hatred...

*They are jealous of your strong character,
your blessed fate, jealous of your husband."*

No consideration of sending the children out of
the room in this private adult moment crosses
Elena's mind: there is no cleft between adult life
and childhood here; jealously and hatred and their
power are daily realities to these young children.

"Make her better, Mamma, make my Zia better!"
implores Irene.

Now stopping the kneading at the sides of
Teresa's head, the wise woman puts her left hand
over the young woman's forehead, gently pushing,
more guiding, her head into the cradle formed by
her forearm and elbow.

Still incanting, she softly encourages Teresa to
open her eyes and look into the waters below.

"May this malicious spell be removed from this poor innocent girl;

May it be broken and dissolve and return to the evil one from which it issued."

"In nomine Patris et Filii et Spiritus Sancti,"

prays Elena, simultaneously making a four-pointed sign of the Holy Cross over the dish and the water it contains.

Three times she draws this sacred symbol of power over the bone-white plate.

Thereafter, with her right hand, Elena takes a drop of thick golden oil of olives, an anointing unguent, onto the tip of her forefinger.

Beyond the line of Teresa's sight, but near the water, she lets the heavy droplet slip, slip thickly, unctuous onto the surface of the almost warm fluid, where it remains surface-tensioned intact, integral…

... for a brief infinitesimal second, before bursting-breaking into an iridescent spread across the liquid surface of the ablutive waters in the dish.

Irene – an ancient self-composure and wisdom appearing on her tiny face -- has now moved closer to the women, closest to her aunt, who looks exhausted but delivered and more relieved.

Tears are streaming down her Aunt's face.

Elements of the exorcism have been indelibly engraved on the girl-child's developing mind and memory.

The two-year-old puts her cheek on her aunt's cheek, wet with the salty waters of relief, and cradles it in her chubby miniature hands.

Elena moves off gently from her patient, away to the stove, and begins warming the nutritious chicken broth and pastina she has prepared ...

... to restore Teresa back to her former strength and energy.

Teresa kisses the redolent top of Irene's little head, summons her strength, rises, still unsteady, wobbly, and removes the ceremonial vessels from the table, washes them, and sets the table for their light midday meal.

Even her weakness does not allow for disrespect and laziness in another's home.

At this point, Luigi came into the room as if entering a holy sanctuary, unsummoned, but knowing intuitively that the ceremony had been completed, reticent and respectful of the feminine energy that had transpired between the two women.

... Perhaps, too, a wisp of the bubbling chicken broth had wafted out to him.

He silently opens the shutters of a window to let in the afternoon air and light.

Teresa stayed and broke bread with Elena, Luigi, and the children.

She ate slowly and carefully, so as not to over-strain her stomach after the fast and the casting away of the Malocchio.

Elena had made a special *dolce* of white-ricotta filled cannoli, with a small cup of piping hot espresso and the cherished sugar that was, together with coffee, slowly becoming more and more available, before Teresa, released and strengthened, would start her way back to Monteforte Cilento and another *pranzo-cena* with her own son and family.

Luigi goes out to the smoothed-flagstone, apron-area in front of their home to enjoy some postprandial *Strega* – the yellow, sweet, herb-filled liqueur that is so popular in these parts – and smoke the remainder of his crooked, self-rolled cigar.

The women remain in the kitchen to tidy up.

Elena and Teresa discuss mundane matters, then the wise-woman prepares a special packet of salami, viscuotti, and some confetti for the boys, to take with her.

Luigi, just a bit later, before his sister's departure, will add further to her welcomed fardels with a few light bundles of fatwood.

Elena and Teresa's eyes meet, and the senior woman puts her hand, unnoticed by her husband, gently and lovingly onto her sister-in-law's abdomen … as an unspoken prophesy that Pasqualino would not be her last child.

CHAPTER 14

Giambone comes forward from the shadows where he had been and holds back some vines to make himself clearly seen to the boys, not wanting to frighten them in these, to them, unfamiliar surroundings.

Where the ridge dividing the *nuraghe-* and beehive-dotted forest, on the one side, from the glen with its orchards and animals on the other, where it joined a larger flank of Monte Chianiello, Pasqualino and Giuseppe, now following Mimma toward her Master, saw that they were approaching what seemed to be a large foliage covered opening, a man-sized hole in the stone of the mountainside.

It is straight ahead of them on the ridge, a small waterfall coming from further up the hill, flowing down the side of the mountain, crossing in a small stream just in front of this "entrance".

Animals and humans can easily ford or simply jump over this natural moat.

The top of this ridge leading to the cave and the main entrance to the cave itself are not visible from the path several hundred meters away and below through the forest, the path Monteforte's villagers take to Capizzo and Magliano Vetere and vice versa.

Following the meandering path of this very same small waterfall backwards, up the mountain, Lino spies a second, smaller opening above and to the left of the main access to the old man's dwelling.

This "window" is almond-shaped and is covered by this very same waterfall, somewhat larger, wider here.

From behind and through this small opening, Giambone's redirects the fresh cool mountain water during the wet season into his cave with cane-reed pipes -- *Arundo Donax*, into a carved basin of stone.

The larger – actually *larger-than-a man* -- "mouth", the main opening into his cave, was naturally and "artificially" nasconded behind hanging brush and bosky vegetation.

Giambone lives, has lived for many years, hermit-like, in this grotto on a flank of Monte Chianiello above Monteforte Cilento. Only infrequently did he make his way down to the village itself anymore; perhaps only two or three times a year.

******

Pasqualino Acquaviva and Giuseppe Rossi arrived underneath a shaded atrium below the rocky ledge overhanging the principal entrance to Giambone's *Grotta*, where the boys first heard and then saw that there were rabbit and guinea pig hutches on what seemed to be wheels or rollers made of wood, so that this sylvan Noah could take them further inside when the weather became too inclement or uncomfortable, or to protect them from dangers both human and animal.

The small furry creatures squealed and scampered as the two boys approached, throwing up hay-dust with their diminutive feet and bits of dry grass and grain husks into the air, Giuseppe stretching himself up on tiptoes to view them better.

Upon entering the cave, it took the boys a few seconds for their eyes to accustom to the diminished light streaming in through green vegetation and flowing water.

Gradually, more and more of the old hermit's abode came into focus.

The boys were in awe when they began to perceive the internal, almost cathedral-like space of Giambone's home...not only because of the size and mysteriousness of the place, but because it was accoutered with so many things that they were not used to: books, lots of books, tomes whose titles they were unable to read; small birds twittering in cages; a large stone hearth in the center...and yet other things they could either not recognize or remained yet to be discovered.

The two are overwhelmed, staring quietly about them, enthralled.

Giuseppe moves first as his curiosity always overcomes his caution, wandering from one side of the large furnished space to the other, in a kind of greedy interest … while Pasqualino continues to view everything from his fixed focal point, moving his eyes and head around in as much of a complete circle as he could manage, then slowly back.

Almost as if returning to his senses, Pasqualino realizes what his little cousin is doing:

"Pèppe, come back to me. It's not polite, what you are doing!" he whispers as if in a holy place, yet firmly, commandingly.

The Giambone smiles and calms them both when he defuses the taut propriety of the elder boy,

"Don't worry, children. It's perfectly in order. Feel free to walk around. Nothing is dangerous except for my shotgun, and it isn't loaded at the moment."

"Also, don't open any of the cages or my pets will run away, and the dogs and I will have to try to get them back!"

They still did not move for a moment --
wondering what he meant by "dogs" --, still
mesmerized, their perceptions ensnared by the
wonders around them, until the spell was broken
again by the Giambone asking them cordially,

"Nu pocc' re té?" – they understand him, but he
has a funny way of lilting their dialect.

Lacking Pasqualino's restricting propriety and
respectfulness, more naturally outgoing, Pèppe went
and found a spot for himself to sit down on, to the
other side of the hearth, on a low-lying divan,
covered in the skins of sheep and goats.

The lads hadn't noticed the second dog before,
now sitting up after being curled comfortably in a
basket, to the side of the divan:

... a small aging gray-brown greyhound.

"Tripolina, fai a brava!!" spoke the old man firmly
but lovingly to his long-time house guardian.

Tripolina was old and gentle, and she took an
immediate liking to the two boys.

She began slowly jiggling at her spot, wagging her tail excitedly, indeed seeming as if *it* were wiggling all of her, licking her chops and whimpering excitedly, almost tap-dancing with her forepaws.

The company of humans other than her master had been non-existent in her revier for so many years.

Pasqualino goes over to the little dog and hunkers down to pet her and allow her to put her front legs and torso on his lap while she searches greedily for his hands to lick;

Giuseppe has already left the divan and is immediately at his cousin's side to share their joy.

Above this central area of the caverna, the ceiling vaulted up with stony outcroppings reminiscent of gargoyles, into higher spaces, darkened recesses, leading up through the inside of the mountain to where they could not see, the smoke and heat from his stone-hearth being pushed in the opposite direction of gravity by the small warming fire, a fire often necessary even until the beginning of high summer.

Worn old rugs covered the ground and reed-woven floor mats, hand-hewn cabinets along walls, a small low table made of vertical, upright stones, topped with a cross-slice of a large oak in front of the divan served as their tea-table ...

...and what amazed them most, to the left of the main entrance from where they were, against the cave wall ... an ebony black stand-up piano!

Pasqualino and Giuseppe had never seen such an instrument, although they had heard it played on the radio -- accompanying opera arias and patriotic fascist songs -- in the Bar Salerno on the Piazza of Monteforte.

(Legend and rumor maintained that demons had helped the old man transport it up here, but it had simply been his own sinew aided by a cart, goats, heavy ropes, and a donkey.)

Drying sausages, and rolls of heavy-string-webbed wheels of cheese, drying corn and hanging onions and pepperoncini, flasks of dark red and flasks of golden-colored liquids crowded in a corner ... wherever their eyes roved, the boys were treated to a larder of earthly delights.

Rough and aged weights and dumbbells, too, there were in the Giambone's cave.

The three "gentlemen" enjoy some chamomile and peppermint tea with beetroot sugar and hard viscuotti and some hazelnuts and almonds.

****

Over the coming weeks, month-upon-month, through the intensely hot summer and then into the gradually cooling autumn, the boys secretly visit the Giambone on every second Sunday, after obediently attending Mass.

During these weeks, Pasqualino Acquaviva and Giuseppe Rossi get their first "formal", "academic" education.

Each time, for the two odd hours they spend there, the old teacher prepares a "lesson" for them:

– learning the alphabet, how to say words and phrases in "proper" Italian, numerals and simple mathematics, the history of the Greeks and Romans, the Risorgimento, famous Italians, even a few phrases in Latin!

The Giambone taught them the Latin names of all the animals both in his home such as the guinea pigs and the beautiful songbirds – the *cardilli*, as well as of the wild beasts of the forest and mountain.

Education is a luxury these boys do not have, especially in these southern parts of Italy, a region that the Fascists had even used for the internal exile of opponents to their regime, especially leftist intellectuals such as the famous Jewish writer and regime critic Carlo Lèvi.

Children only went to school until, at the very most, the 3rd grade because most of them had to work. Some had the fortune of attending trade schools for becoming masters at such trades as tailoring or shoemaking.

Only the very fewest went on to continue their studics or went to religious Catholic schools in other cities such as Genoa, Savona, Rome…and even these privileges for these few chosen, lucky ones, had become rarer during this grinding, wearying, inhuman war.

Frank A. Merola

CHAPTER 15

The two lads see the Giambone over a period of several months, until one day near the end of September 1944 Mamma returns early because she had forgotten something important for Elena – a small table covering done in the jagged, but beautiful, intricate, medieval *Ricamo d'Assisi* – and, from the corner of her eye notices a standing, alert figure on the boys' pasture, arms outstretched – believing it is Pasqualino, she calls out in greeting.

Getting no response after several attempts, she moves towards him and discovers the scarecrow *"Michele"* …but no boys.

Their goats, in fact the entire herd, were calm and peaceable, Lisetta tied docile and resting to a small pine, enjoying its shade.

At first, she believes they are simply somewhere in the surrounding forests at the fringes of the pasture, perhaps going to the bathroom, and begins calling around her for them.

Still no answer, no Pasqualino, no Giuseppe, even when her calls increased in both volume and frequency, a rising panic begins to grab slowly around her chest, up to her throat.

Where the Devil are they?
she wonders as her eyes scan the area.

The boys hear her calling for them; they were just finishing their time with Giambone and had reached the edge of the ridge to begin their descent back to the flock. Just previously Mimma had begun to bark, as they were taking their leave from their teacher; going outside they hear Mamma's voice.

Giving heed now to Mamma's frantic calls, they begin running down, scrambling as fast as their legs could take them, scrambling through the underbrush, Pasqualino firmly holding onto Giuseppe's hand and almost pulling him through the air behind him!

She sees them ford the brook when she looks behind her on the path from which she had just come…coming out of a copsy area she had expressly told them to avoid…*and* on the wrong side of the stream, no less!

Reaching them, in a panic of love, fear, and anger that she had almost lost her only son and his beloved cousin, she punishes them.

Grabbing them by one arm each, she shakes them, gives them a switching with a stick she finds lying on the ground, in the brush nearby, less in anger than in emotional fear that something had happened to them…and she missed her husband and his fatherly presence…and yells that they will get a sound hiding with a strap once Papá returns home!!!

Teresa orders them to stay with the animals now and bring them home immediately. She will deal with the two reprobates later, when she returns from Magliano Vetere ….

******

Once back again at the home-stalls in Monteforte with their herd, the two worried and guilty miscreants sheepishly, obediently carry out their duties.

Teresa will let her older sister Filomena, Giuseppe's Mom, know of her decision once she returns from Elena and Luigi's. She is shaken to her core to think what might have happened....

Returning back later in the afternoon, she grounds them; their irresponsibility and disobedience are beyond the pale, and the boys are commanded to stay at home and help Nonna around the house with the chickens ... *and* decides to merge the boys' herd with that of Giuseppe's older sisters and brothers.

****

Nonna Domenica respects her daughter's decision, but is troubled by it.

She does not like how Giuseppe and Pasqualino have, subsequent to their "transgression", become very reticent, very downcast, morose and moping at their duties to assist her: their spirit is gone.

However much she tries, she can draw no further information from the boys as to what they had been doing in the forest prior to Mamma-Zia's return.

Even the Rossi youth come to collect Lino and Pèppe's goats silently, respectfully -- having abandoned any thoughts of taunting the lads --, casting surreptitious, pitying sidelong glances at the two boys, both sitting on a rough log bench under the shade of a slate-roofed shed, watching their animals going off up the mountainside without them.

Only the older, middle sister, Domenico's fraternal twin, Francesca has the courage to come over to her little brother and tousle his hair, giving him a quick peck on the cheek.

She simply gently touches Pasqualino's shoulder, he sitting there stoically staring away from her.

A somber pall has descended on the Acquaviva-Rossi farmstead.

****

Frank A. Merola

CHAPTER 16

Several weeks continue in this way, and routine and the positive developments of the war – as sensed through the entire village -- bring a lightening of spirits once again, even to the lads.

It is mid-October and a good harvest is behind them, or is just about to begin for crops such as the grapes and the olives.

Mamma continues with her daily work of bringing back needed resources from Monte Chianiello and visiting her family in the neighboring village.

Too, her heart is lighter with the news that Nunzio would be coming home for a short furlough at the beginning of January – just in time for the *Mercato della Befana* -- the Epiphany Market.

Concern is replaced by grateful relief in the family's hearts —

-- a sniper's bullet had grazed the fleshy part of Nunzio's upper left arm, but had left no further damage other than an ugly scar, as he recounted to them in his latest letter.

A sense of positive anticipation and joy began to fill their homestead.

Nonna Domenica continues her beloved routine of telling the boys stories from the old days in the evenings before they fell asleep – of the *Munaciedd'*, of the *Lupo-Mannaro*, of *streghe* and *stregone*, of giant serpents living in the forest, of strange, mysterious people who could disappear at will, of the *Briganti Capozzoli*, of people who were born at the stroke of midnight on Christmas Eve -- with tails! and many, many more such fascinating accounts.

Her treasure chest of memories seemed limitless, and she took this bedtime ceremony all the more seriously during the boys' "sentence" away from their pasture.

****

Nonna Domenica D'Orsi *in Salerno* loved her grandchildren deeply, limitlessly -- much, much, much more than she would ever let on.

Too, she had a grandparent's calm, cool, fair distance to these grand-offspring that their immediate parents did not.

Thus, she let many things pass in their behavior that she knew from experience were simply the things that kids did, had to do, had to experience and go through...and was in no way ruffled by them.

But, almost unconsciously, little events started to stick in the web of her perception and memory, slowly beginning to snag in the invisible net of her mind, like scraps of a ripped, secret parchment scattered to the winds, now slowly coming together again and forming an important message, a pattern she could not yet recognize....

******

The first such event transpired when she had been scattering some feed corn to the chickens and ducks and Giuseppe had been skipping around in the morning sunlight with some of the younger dogs while they leapt in gleeful play around his little legs:

"Cape Cane! Cape Cane!" she thought she had heard him say.

"No, Pèppe, no…. It's 'Chiapp' ú cann' '
not 'Cape Cane' ", she corrected him in the dialect of the Cilento.

"Va bo, Nó. Va bo!", he had assented after a brief pause of consideration.

"Chiapp ú cann'! Chiapp ú cann'!" he had continued in his gamboling game, prancing and singing as the dogs jumped up to lick him.

She watched him carefully and turned back to feeding the poultry, but something had stuck itself in her cognition, like a small bump in the road of her memory…. something filed away in her subconscious….

A second, a third episode had caught her attention even further while the boys were with her during the days of their "exile" from the flanks of Monte Chianiello:

The second "bump" came while she was carrying a vessel of the water used for washing the food wastes from their dishes, wastewater that she would give to the pigs now fattening in their stalls – it would give them some tasty liquids with a few nutritious tidbits in them.

Pasqualino and Giuseppe were hunkering down near to the dried sandy-mud ground at the side of the stall – doing something there on the hardened earth.

She had not done it on purpose, but they had not heard her approach them with the enameled washing vessel slightly sloshing.

Had Lino just scratched a large "P" in the earth?

...and had begun a second letter?

When they heard her, both boys stood up and directly on the symbols they had been creating, Pasqualino holding the stick behind him.

"What are you up to, boys?" she inquires out of habit, straining a bit under the weight of the water-filled container she held in front of her, balancing it to stop it from sloshing out, to keep from wasting any of its valuable fluid.

"Niente, Nonna. Nothing, Nonna. Pèppe and I were just drawing some figures." Pasqualino replies collectedly, looking directly at her with widened eyes.

"Here, let me hold the pen-gate open for you," and he moves past her to lift the heavy rope holding closed the door to the pigs' area.

Giuseppe moves to where Lino had been standing and squiggles with his shoes over the earth that his older cousin had just been etching in, thereby smearing the figures, patting the images down back into the wet, softened earth and sand.

This, too, seemed odd to her....

As she walked on into the pigs' pen, she spontaneously remembered some smeared figures made of fire-charcoal ash on the flagstones around the farm, rubbed away, like the smeared ashes on foreheads after Ash Wednesday.

Her suspicions were piqued even further, and she wondered again what were those two little scoundrels up to???

She knew both of them probably better than they knew themselves…and something was afoot.

The penultimate piece of the puzzle came when she observes and hears the boys playing together and speaking a few words in High Italian, like two actors from a *Truppa di Commedia* and wonders where they had picked it up.

Perhaps they were simply imitating Padre Massimiliano's words from his sermons and his masses…but he normally only used ecclesiastical language, predominantly Church Latin…not these theatrical renderings.

Unwilled, for some perhaps suppressed reason, Domenica's mind presented her a mind-image of another person who used to speak so clearly the chosen Florentine of United Italy....

Nonna does not give away her advantage but decides now to keep a closer, more focused, more suspicious eye on these two young gentlemen.

The key to unlocking the mystery is presented to her once when she approaches the boys' sleeping straw cot in the middle of the large common room of her home and notices Pasqualino pushing something under their bed with his foot.

Initially, she assumes it is Pasqualino and Giuseppe's shoes because that is where they are stored when they are not in use.

Nonna Domenica decides on her plan of action for that evening.

****

That night for their precious, special ritual she recounts to them a story of the *"Cascate dei Capelli di Venere"* – *The Falls of Venus' Tresses* when the goddess Aphrodite punished a poor shepherd youth lovestruck by her beauty.

Pasqualino and Giuseppe sat up on their straw cot and leant their backs against the wall of Nonno Francesco's small home.

They were all eyes and ears ready to imagine, to capture every single word Nonna told them of these ancient stories.

Nonna Domenica began, sitting on the wicker-woven chair her brother Donato had made for her, drawing it nearer, closer to the lads' bed.

"One day Venus, or Aphrodite as the Greeks called her, decided to go to a small glen in the mountains, to a small green oasis to refresh herself from the heat of the day and find some peace and restoration.

The goddess loved that place; she had made it her secret little garden, her personal paradise.

Every time she felt the need to be alone, whenever she wanted to simply rest, she went there and stretched out on the soft green mosses to listen to the noises of nature surrounding it and her, to breathe in the redolent, intoxicating fragrances.

One fine day, by chance, a simple human shepherd found himself passing through those areas while seeking more delectable pastures for his flock and noticed a beautiful, long-tressed girl dancing with abandon.

An obsessive infatuated love overtook him.

A single glance, and he fell madly in love, he was enraptured, but it was not a gentle and simple love: it was a blinding obsession that possessed the very fibers of his being.

Every day thereafter, in fact, he went near the grove and hid behind a tree, spending hours spying on Venere, taking in every glimpse of her as if it were the only food he needed to live.

In particular, the young man was struck by the sylph's hair: blond, as he had never seen, similar to gold, long and light, as soft as silk. She seemed like a celestial being.

He wanted those locks more than anything else he had ever wanted in his short young life.

And it was under this enthralling magic, consumed and possessed by this uncontrollable desire that, one night, he decided to creep up secretly to this angelic girl and cut off a lock of her wonderous hair while she was asleep."

Giuseppe has now wiggled his way forward and is sitting in front of Pasqualino, who holds his cousin around his small torso to him, while the two of them sit cross-legged and rapt in attention; Pèppe is twirling a curl of his own ginger hair, a little lock to the left of his forehead, with his left hand.

*"Aphrodite, Venere, has greater powers than mere mortals, and, so, obviously, senses the presence of the shepherd youth even in her sleep, and awakens with a **start**!"*

The lads draw slightly back at this dramatic moment as Nonna emphasizes the "start" with her body, moving her face suddenly forward, closer towards them, widening her crystal green eyes at the same time.

*"The Dea saw her attacker slinking away with her hair
and angrily decided not to let him get away with his crime!*

*Immediately, she metes out her revenge onto this
unsuspecting, callow youth!*

*The shepherd, in fact, after running for a couple of meters,
no longer feels the silken shimmering strands of the goddess
Venus' locks in his hands,*

*… but rather her golden hair has turned suddenly into
water, only water, now flowing away, slipping uncontrollably
through his calloused hand and fingers.*

He watched helplessly: it could not be held back!"

The boys had caught and held their breaths at
this magical transformation – water held dark fears
of death for them.

They knew nothing of swimming.

Accounts of children drowning even in the
irrigation canals watering the artichoke and tomato
fields between the River Sele and Paestum down
below on the littoral plain were, tragically, …

…not unknown…not to speak of the drownings in rivers and the *Mare Nostrum*.

"The shepherd boy realized in growing panic that these swiftly streaming waters could not be held back.

This water, rather, increased more and more in volume the more he tried to grasp and hold it in his mortal fingers.

Gradually, it filled the small glen beloved to Aphrodite and began to overtake him, to reach under his chin, and finally to drown the careless, hapless shepherd, who could not swim. Taking a final breath, he was lost to the waves.

Thus did the deity punish him by turning the golden strands into a raging flood that drags him down to his death."

Nonna pauses an instant for dramatic effect, looking from one boy to the other.

She continues:

"Venus, who, nevertheless, was not a wicked deity, softened at hearing the dying screams of that young boy and decided to give him an opportunity for his soul's eternal salvation.

Seeing what her act of vengeance had wrought when she heard his dying cries, now realizing that his love had been true and pure even until the end, but no longer being able to rescind the sentence and penalty she had spoken for his transgression — as even the gods must follow the law once it has been declared — she was now overcome with sorrow, filled with regret at what she had done to this poor, befoibled human.

Considering all of this afterwards, she decides to mitigate the pain she had caused and, yet, not break her decree:

The lovely goddess Venus turns the area into a beautiful place of quiet beauty graced with a waterfall whose individual rivulets are so fine and gossamer that they are reminiscent of her hair.

The shepherd's spirit she allowed to dwell within a lovely plant, The Maidenhair Fern, that only grew in this glen, to be always near to her and enjoy for eternity the gossamer, finely-streamed waterfalls born of her silken strands of hair.

Thus, did she keep the youth close to her, honor his desire and courage and, thus, too, lessen the pain on his immortal soul of the sentence for his act of stealing."

Nonna places her hands now, palm-down, on her laps and remains silent for a moment, looking unblinkingly at her two grandsons with her liquid green eyes, which could have been the pools of Aphrodite's verdant mossy secret Shangri-La.

Pasqualino shakes himself to come back into reality.

Pèppe asks,

"Is the hair-water place here in the mountains, Nonna?"

"Peppino, perhaps … there are small falls and hidden areas on Monte Chianiello, but this one I've told you about is further to the south of Monteforte, in the village of Casaletto Spartano -- it was so that the Cascate dei Capelli di Venere were born there, a place still steeped in magic and beauty and mystery – like the Goddess herself."

Nonna kisses both of them, and they lay themselves down to sleep, prayers and the Sign of the Cross made over their young bodies and souls, after-images of her tales filling their heads.

****

The boys are fast asleep after their cherished, anticipated time with their Nonna Domenica and her beloved tales.

Nonno Francesco has not yet returned from his social time with the other menfolk of Monteforte at the Bar Salerno;

Amongst them is Nonno Pasquale Acquaviva, Nunzio's father…events were overtaking each other rapidly as the War moved steadily, grindingly North, to the very heart of the Teutonic homeland …

… hope of an impending end were growing, but ploddingly slow: a second foothold and advances had been attempted that June in Normandy, in occupied France, during that other D-Day, on other beaches drenched in vivid russet, far to the Northwest of Operation Avalanche, once again with the accompanying grueling, piteous, heart-rending massive loss of lives.

… yet, too, these second footholds had held, as they were finally holding now in Italy.

Earlier in the War, when the Germans sensed the political tide turning in Italy, some of these older gentlemen had been conscripted into munitions factories in Germany, even as far as Berlin itself.

Not all had returned.

One of the Nicolettis, Elena's father, had even brought back a tiny, intricate, filigreed hair-clasp in the shape of a delicate butterfly for his grand-daughter: a thing of singular beauty he had found during his sentence in the capital of the Third Reich.

Closer to home, here in Italy the U.S. Fifth Army had captured Monte Battaglia on the Nazi-held, appropriately-named Gothic Line, helped by the Italian partisans of *la Resistenza* after a four-day battle ... – ... had Francesco Salerno's son-in-law, Pasquale Acquaviva's son Nunzio been with them?

Further battles were taking place in offensive attacks launched toward Bologna and La Spezia, attacks that will end in a month with heavy losses and a limited gain of ground.

The Forces of the British Eighth Army had launched successful attack maneuvers beyond the river Rubicon – the Italians knowing in their hearts what grave significance this meant for the Germans, for no lesser than the great Julius Caesar himself had known it so many centuries ago.

Soldiers even from a land at the other end of the world, Nuova Zelanda, were fighting side-by-side with their Italian boys, helping, the gentlemen elders of Monteforte Cilento recounted in grateful amazement to each other.

Marshall Badoglio was out; the Allies officially recognized the Italian government under Ivanoe Bonomi.

This latter had finally decided to take on the position of the new Prime Minister of a free Italy under a barrage of convincing, motivating, overwhelming persuasion from Winston Churchill's rhetoric.

****

Nonna is now able to put her resolution into action, to solve the conundrum nagging at her, and reaches under the boys' bed as they soundly slept; initially, expectedly, she touches merely the boys' diminutive shoes.

Then, as her hand moves silently left and right and deeper underneath, in the darkness, feels something slightly rough and square and wooden, with metal clasps and a small metal handle.

Pulling it out ever so quietly from behind the collection of children's footwear, ever, ever so gently, Nonna recognizes in her hands a small elegantly made but robust, wooden cigar box with a closed, hinged, dual-clasped top:

An old cigar box from the *Tabacchificio Fiocche*, located near the River Sele -- on a triangulation southeast of Battipaglia and southwest of Eboli --, with the name of the famed tobacco factory branded in an elegant, older script into its cover.

During the War, the Tabacchificio had been transformed into a cannery to supply food for the military and the civilian populace;

… now it was nothing more than a mass of bombed-out rubble, distorted iron, a few jagged walls.

She opens the wooden top and slips back the additional thin lid underneath, through its carefully notched tracks, and discovers little stone and wood carved objects in this protected space --

-- of horned sheep, goats, chimeras, bears, wolves, lions, serpents, dragons, tiny images of seated goddesses;

In it, too, were religious and pagan amulets, trinkets, worn paper images of the Saints, even some dried garlic and chili peppers -- *pepperoncini.*

There is a child-fist sized pomegranate in red-stone and – most surprisingly – a tiny beehive of bees' wax, slightly flattened at the apex, and something carved from a shiny black stone, like a tiny dome, with an all-seeing eye on it near the top.

Nonna has to smile to herself when she finds a single remaining confetto, almost like a reserved war-ration, amongst the other treasures.

A tear rolls unexpectedly from her eye onto the accumulated treasures of her grandboys.

Now the disjointed pieces of the puzzle form clearly the image she had sensed they might.

She is certain....

She replaces the treasure chest and its sacred contents back to the very place she had found it, behind the protective camouflage of the lads' shoes.

Domenica knows what she must do.

****

The next day, Domenica takes her daughter aside while the younger woman is washing the family laundry by hand at the fountain in the piazza.

"Terè, I need to talk to you about the boys," she begins, always referring to the two cousins as if they belonged together, as if they were brothers.

As she recounts what she has discovered to
Teresa, she pleads gently with her, trying to
convince her to let the boys continue tending their
goats on the mountainside…and to continue
visiting the man she referred to as *"Dottore di Lucca"*
– he had been her teacher for a short time in her
youth and was well-educated.

He had also been a respected physician in
Monteforte for many years before his withdrawal,
his retreat into the forested slopes of the Mountain.

Too, he had been a good friend and comrade of
her brother Donato during the Great War.

Domenica knew the value of education and knew
the quality of the man instructing her grandsons.

Teresa followed her Mother's words carefully,
weighing them in her heart; she had heard of this
reclusive doctor-teacher, a man the townsfolk
referred to as *"il Giambone"* because of his strong,
stocky stature and knew that he had been her
Mother's teacher for a short time, many, many years
ago in the evenings when Domenica's parents had
let her go…but then something had happened.

Education was so very scarce for the children of Monteforte and some long for it almost as if it were The Very Water of Life.

Nonna Domenica continues to impress upon her daughter the importance of gaining an education.

Inside her heart, the younger woman is glowingly moved by this chance these children could have.

Too, Teresa Acquaviva is secretly proud of their cleverness and their "rebellion", their dissembling foxiness, without being able to put it into words, furthering the masculinity of these boys, as it had been done by mothers in these Southern regions for generations, centuries before … they had been able to fool even her for several months, and the use of Arcangelo Michele was a truly crafty, dissembling trick, and the deception had worked.

Finally, Teresa agrees, acquiesces.

Later that very day she grills Pasqualino and Giuseppe until they finally admit what they had done, that they had been visiting the *Giambone* and what he had been teaching them.

In a flood of release, Giuseppe begins bubbling out about all of the wonders of the grotta – its animals, its books, even a *pianoforte!*

Teresa, however, remains distant, stern, and aloof at the red-head's joyful accounts, like one of the Fates herself, judging a mere mortal, arms folded tightly, magisterially over her breast.

Looking down upon them with an air of juridical gravitas, she informs the two seemingly repentant convicts of their commuted sentence…but severely warns them – with threats of sound whippings by both her and her husband -- to be careful.

To not seem too lenient, Mamma-Zia orders them, in addition to tending their own herds and other current responsibilities, that they must also carry wood-logs into the house for their Nonna, feed the chickens, ducks, and other fowl daily, bring in the eggs safely to Nonna, and, on Sundays, say ten Our Fathers and ten Hail Marys on their knees *before* they can leave the Church.

****

Nonno Francesco Salerno is not burdened with these questions of upbringing but does notice now how motivated and eager, happier, Lino and Pèppe seem to be with the herds and their additional duties.

He is glad that he no longer has to worry about them while his son-in-law is fighting in the liberating army with the *partigiani* and Allies, and he was never one to want to deal with difficulties and conflicts, preferring to sit in and around the Bar Salerno with his compatriots, smoking their now more frequent American cigarettes, discussing about God and the World, while drinking wine, *liquori,* and *amari.*

Thus, it continued thereafter, every second Sunday, that Pasqualino Acquaviva and Giuseppe Rossi could recommence with their visits to their hermit-teacher.

Teresa and Nonna would make *viscuotti, taralle,* and for the Advent season, honey-coated *struffoli* for the aged Giambone as a thanks for his efforts at educating the young "students".

As the war waned and the tides turned even more massively against the Germans, and with local agricultural production rebounding, food slowly became more abundant and various as in the old times and traditions, thus bringing back the small joys of normalcy that had been absent for so long.

Sometimes the ladies added a small basket or a burlap sack laden with bottled olive oil and tomato conserves, dried oregano – even though he had his own spice garden in the glen -- and an occasional *salame di cinghiale,* made an especially bounteous gift for *il Dottore di Lucca.*

For his part, he would send the boys back with quail's eggs wrapped in cloth and buffered in straw or with some of the delicate spices he grew such as thyme, sage, rosemary, lemon-balm, marjoram.

Once in that October of 1944, Mamma becomes worried when the villages in the Cilento are shaken by a light but noticeable earthquake. Mercifully, the tremors cause nothing more than some small, minor rockfalls and pots and pictures falling from their shelves.

Up in the grotta, the dogs began howling moments before the boys and their tutor feel something like a gargantuan subterranean swimming beast flowing through the very stone of the mountain, rolling as it passes under the soles of their feel, like the hump of a massive whale smoothly breaking the surface of the ocean and then going languidly back under the waves.

******

The old man is secretly delighted that his avid, eager students had returned.

He had been wondering what had become of his pupils over the weeks of their absence and had even gone down to their pastures once to look for them. Instead, he found there two teenagers tending their flocks and had inquired as to the lads' whereabouts.

"They need to stay closer to the farm to help their Nonna and to tend the pigs and chickens, Signore," the eldest of the Rossi progeny, Emilia, and the most responsible and dependable amongst them, had replied.

Vittorio moves away, ostensibly to go and attend to a small kid at the further reach of the pasture.

Her answer and her brother's behavior had made him suspicious, especially how she looked away to the side when she recounted this, but he had read out of her words that they were safe and sound, but something else must have transpired....

The Giambone simply looks at her, nods briefly, then moves back up the path returning into the forests.

CHAPTER 17

"Cave canem!"

… Giambone would warn them when they were lovingly attacked and licked by the friendly Mimma and even Tripolina seemed to regain her past puppiness whenever the boys visited.

Every visit, a different theme, a different subject, a different challenge.

They would draw the letters he taught them in a clayey part of the spacious cave that they could then cover over again with a handful of the softened argillaceous earth.

Slowly Lino and Pèppe began to decipher the titles of the innumerable tomes in Dottore di Lucca's library –

… Pasqualino was the faster of the two, but Giuseppe was strongly motivated to catch up, given his natural competitiveness toward his older cousin.

The Giambone's rough-hewn bookshelves held such ponderous, heady works as: *Medicina Umana, Anatomia, La Storia dei Greci e dei Romani, Dante, il Gattopardo, il Corano, La Sacra Bibbia, Il Capitale* – and many others whose titles they could not interpret.

Understanding what the contents held or meant was still a distant hurdle for the children, although they loved to turn the pages to see the beauty and occasional terror of the prints and the lithographs – some were even in color!

Sometimes the old Teacher recounts to them stories from the ancient times, from the Greek and Roman pantheon, of the nobility of their forefathers and foremothers. He tells them of the heroic accounts of famous brigands who fought for Garibaldi and the subsequent unification of the Italian Republic, *il Risorgimento.*

A yellowing Sardinian Flag with the four blindfolded Moors on the white-and-red Cross of Saint George stands proudly near his hearth.

Some of these tales were difficult for them, but the boys liked the images of strong heroes fighting against evil forces, to be with them vicariously, a swelling pride filling their young breasts.

So, so many books! And then there was that large black wooden box, taller than the both of them, with black and white rectangles on it – a *pianoforte*, he had told them.

While they did their alphabet exercises, he would smoke a crooked, hand-rolled cigar, more of a stogie, actually, made from his own tobacco.

He had always been self-sufficient: the supply of cigarettes and cigars from the Fiocche plant down on the plain between the River Sele and Battipaglia had long been stopped by the *Fascisti* to convert the site and its facilities into a tomato-cannery, even well before finally being destroyed by the Allied landings that previous Autumn. The Germans had holed up in this strategic complex of buildings, making it a veritable hell for the young Allied American and British soldiers -- and had caused many casualties before the forces of *die Wehrmacht* were routed and retreated further North.

The smoke from his scraggly, uneven cigar never bothered them as it rose up and up and up into the myriad hidden passageways above the living spaces of the cave, possibly finally joining the swirling winds of the *Varco* at the top of Mount Chianiello.

Chickens roamed around freely in his abode during the day, to pick at any small noisome insects a human eye would have difficulty spotting, such as fleas or mites or bedbugs that might be about.

Their lessons never lasted more than two hours as he was docent-strict to tell them to get back to their herds, as it would be irresponsible should anything happen to them, and he did not want to teach them disobedience.

There were moments of music, too.

Some pieces he had written himself, others were works by the great composers, all played for them on the *pianoforte*, now aging into a dilapidating, rickety standup.

He could now still tune and repair it only so far.

Nevertheless, the melodies that emanated from it were magical – Verdi's *Va Pensiero*, arias and pieces from the operas and the classics, and a song that was very moving and mysterious, whose title Lino could start to read after an effort: *"Per Elisa"*.

The melodies reminded the boys of the tunes that came out of the few radios in the village, but much clearer, much more enchanting, alive, marrow-moving, and beautiful.

Sometimes, he would even let the boys try their hands at playing a simple scale themselves.

Giuseppe, especially, sometimes got carried away with banging on the keys too enthusiastically, too cacophonously, bringing a delighted grin to Pasqualino's face and drawing a laugh out of The Giambone, who then politely encouraged his young charge to be a bit more gentle. *"There was a wrestler in the boy!"* the old gentlemen thought to himself and smiled.

Legend had it that he had made a pact with the Devil who helped him transport it from Sardinia, from his family's home of comparative wealth and nobility up to the cave on Monte Chianiello.

"People will gossip and say I had demons fly this piano up the mountain, but it was simply the strength of myself and my animals and the sturdiness of my cart," he once recounted to them.

The truth was that he had had it transported from Caprera on Sardegna and was all that he had left of his family and their Savoyard fortunes and honor – that, the *Bandiera di Sardegna,* and the miniature nuraghe he made to dot his sylvan realm.

He also showed them how to use herbs and plants and soils to heal wounds and bind them properly.

Once when Giuseppe chased after Tripolina -- temporarily and excitedly having a bout of youthfulness in the presence of the sparky little boy -- into a darkened corner of the grotta, the ginger mop-top uncovered an old black-and-white photograph of a prim and pretty young woman;

… her hair tied back in a proper bun, the image fading from age, on a lower shelf behind a chair next to his straw bed on the homemade wooden slats.

"Zia Teresa!" Giusi exclaims and stands immobile, forgetting Tripolina, concentrating on the image.

Pasqualino, too, having now come over to stand next to his inquisitive cousin, to see what he had discovered, recognizes his mother's features in the picture – yet there was something different in the face, something old-fashioned about her hair, about the clothes she wore.

"Tripolina! Vieni qui!" Giambone calls lovingly to the aged guardian of his home.

The skinny, little hound turns around and runs through the boys' legs, obediently to her master... followed by the lads, who are drawn to her as if by an unseen magnetic force.

Their attention to the image they had seen is dissolved, as if an intoxicating, captivating fog had been blown away from around them.

On more than one occasion *il Giambone* would accompany them to the bend from which he had appeared to them that first day when his little kid was the brunt of the aggressions of the boys' flock Emperors.

In the meantime, too, the Giambone had helped his piebald ram-kid befriend the old buck and the herd queen with her scions, so that he was amicably welcomed or simply ignored whenever he entered into their area.

During their times together with the old teacher, they learn that he has christened his goat *Faunus*.

Later that afternoon, after the boys have returned to their herd, the Giambone goes back to this shelf and puts the image Giuseppe and Pasqualino had been fascinated by down on its face, respectfully, gently, tenderly, after gazing at it for a brief instant, then covers it with one of his handkerchiefs.

****

Simply being in the grotta was an education for the two cousins. Pasqualino and Giuseppe seemed to always discover something new both outside in his fields and inside within the reaches of the elderly physician-scholar's home:

Grazing in the protected glen, behind the approach-ridge to his cave, were Giambone's miniature, black donkey, Vittoria Emanuela, and a she-goat, Benita, with the old, randy billy-goat, Adolfo, and their three kids – Josef, Winston, and Franklin.

Faunus was there with them, too, gamboling about.

When he wasn't playing his piano, the front part of the cave chamber nearest the great mouth-like opening was filled with the songs and twitterings of the little songbirds that he had captured himself with special traps, held in tiny cages: the brightly-multi-colored, red-masked European goldfinches – "*cardilli*", *carduelis carduelis*.

The warm thermals leading up to the *Varco Cervone* drew large rapturous birds: falcons, eagles, and hawks floating, gliding silently, dangerously through them, eyeing for prey.

Of course, foxes and weasels slinked around the forest and near the cave, but they were no match for Tripolina's still keen sense of smell and pin-sharp teeth and Mimma's speed and bear-trap bite.

The rabbits, the *cunigli suricini*, the chickens and quail are kept in raised coops, with inverted metal-flashing hoods on the legs to prevent any climbing up by the feral, wily, meat-eaters…coops just near the entrance of the grotta, under the ledge, where Mimma has her bed of straw, her guard post, always under her protective watch.

Mimma's precinct was outside; Tripolina's inside.

****

Always, before the boys left, they would have a quick bite together with the Giambone, an afternoon "*merendina*" from his natural larder… as was befitting of cultured scholars and gentlemen.

"*An army travels on its stomach, my boys!*", he would always say to them, winking impishly.

They had such treats as dried *uva fragola* – from which he made a weak wine for himself, drinks of "coffee" made from grains, lightened with goat-milk, sweetened by the sugar he extracted from beetroot.

(For his own, "medicinal" purposes, he distilled wild schnapps, *"Grappa"* from either the skins of the grapes he had made wine from or even from his staple-starch potatoes.)

Too, they enjoyed the fruits of the forests, eating the delectable *pignoli,* the delicious white inside of the pine nut and getting blackened, purple fingers in the process of extracting them from their hard shells with rocks.

Giambone made rabbit salamis as a source of meat protein that would nourish him during the cooler winter months because pigs were too difficult to keep on the slope of the mountain. Too, these sausages also kept well during the hot summer in the cave's dry coolness.

Canning of carrots, eggplants, artichokes, tomatoes, peppers; drying of his spices and garlic and onions and *pepperoncini,* apples and pears, guaranteed his health and survival.

******

Dottore di Lucca loved teaching the boys and passing on his knowledge to them.

Yet, as much as he was able -- and gladly and volubly able -- to pass on a small part of his accumulated knowledge to them, so much so was he reticent about his own private past and never mentioned a word of it to anyone.

How he had survived this Second War -- and what had transpired in his life before, all the way back to the Great War – he kept to and for himself, wrapped within the secrecy of his reclusiveness.

The boys were, in any case, far too young for such things and, with the years, the Giambone had become comfortable with himself and felt no need, no urge, no compunction to burden others with his story.

And neither did Donato D'Orsi nor his younger sister Domenica….

CHAPTER 18

The D'Orsis were a good, moderately patrician family with the air of dignity of a lost nobility, and their views were very conservative – for King and Country and then for the Duce, whom the King had initially accepted and legitimized.

The vestiges of this faded social standing and prestige sometimes gave Domenica, and especially her daughter Teresa, an air of haughtiness and prideful self-respect.

Sic transit gloria mundi.

The first Sunday of Advent was approaching, and Mother and Daughter were sitting, doing *Ricamo d'Assisi* by the fire in the common room of their home, when Domenica sensed it was time to tell Teresa of what had happened those many years ago.

Nonno Francesco was still out and the boys had been tucked away and thereafter fallen asleep, holding each other.

Teresa had sensed something in her mother ever since she had convinced her to let the boys continue to visit the mysterious old man of the mountain…

-- she knew that her Mother loved Francesco Salerno, and he had been a good father – even though quite easy-going and sociable, preferring to be in discussions with his friends at the *Bar Salerno,* sipping an *amaro* and smoking, he was not drunken, womanizing, and brutal like the men in some of the other families.

Nevertheless, Teresa sensed in her woman's breast that all of her Mother's embers had not yet died out for this *"Giambone"*, that something had transpired those so many years ago.

Teresa listened quietly and attentively, waiting for every word from her Mother's mouth, in parallel continuing to work on her needlepoint.

Domenica tells her about the *Giambone*, a story that began on the island of Sardegna, in the final years of the *Ottocento*, before the Great War, when Domenica herself was just a small girl in Monteforte Cilento.

Domenica's brother Donato, 12 years her senior, had been sent proudly by their parents to join the elite troops of the *"Granatiere di Sardegna"*.

Giuseppe di Lucca's family had come from Sardegna, from the island of Caprera, an island in the northeast of the larger island, just southwest of Corsica, and were related to the House of Savoy.

He was an only child.

Giuseppe had completed his medical training with the highest honors at the University of Sassari and was now a doctor-in-training, a medic, as it were, for the fighting men of the Sardinian Grenadiers.

Strangely, though, Donato and Giuseppe first met on the sands and sawdust of the Roman wrestling pit of the troop's barracks.

Dottore di Lucca, as he was addressed by the recruits, though an excellent student and medic, needed the balance to his intellectual pursuits provided by the ring and its competitive, strenuous, sometimes brutal physical struggles, to keep his naturally strong and muscular body in form.

Donato D'Orsi was tall for a Southern Italian, over one-ninety, and had always loved physical exertion in a natural way.

Donato had been undefeated in this ancient discipline until that one afternoon when a short wiry fellow was able to throw his massive weight and height down onto his back onto the sawdust-softened sand of the pit after only a few feints and parries.

At first he did not recognize the regiment's doctor without his white lab coat, but became aware of who he was only when they were in hand-to-hand struggle, grunting and grimacing, straining, eyeball-to-eyeball.

They became close friends and comrades thereafter.

Despite their differences in appearance and widely differing political views, the two became inseparable.

After his 2 years of intense military training, Donato returned to Monteforte to continue working in their family's carpentry and masonry shop near the entrance to Monteforte, on the mountain-hugging road from Trentinara; Giuseppe remains on Sardegna to complete the final year of his internship.

Wanting a change, a new beginning after his medical studies were completed, Giambone confides his desires, his unease to his friend in a letter. Donato convinces his medical, wrestling companion to come down to Monteforte Cilento: Giuseppe could assist the village's aging physician, Dottore Gorga, with his patients.

Too, as an added benefit to the Montefortese, he could try his hand at teaching the interested children of various grades and abilities; Monteforte Cilento had no proper teacher.

Giuseppe di Lucca followed his friend's advice and arrived in August of 1902 to the relative poverty of this mountain village of the Mezzogiorno.

While there, he stayed in a simple room at the home of an aged widow that was known locally as "*Mammarella*".

Donato's younger sister Domenica was 13 at the time.

With his modern, advanced training and his natural intelligence, Dottore di Lucca quickly became a respected doctor and beloved teacher in the hearts and homes of Monteforte.

Whenever he was with Doctor Gorga, however, he always showed the requisite honor, humility, and respect to this long-time physician of the town.

He applied his more modern techniques and knowledge in such a way as to make the more senior medical man feel that the ideas had come from himself and not from the younger man.

School was in the evenings because children had to work for their families during the day, and it was held in the left transept of the Chiesa di Santa Maria Assunta at the heart of Monteforte.

As a grateful thanks to the villagers of Monteforte, Giuseppe had had his black standup *pianoforte* transported all the way from Caprera to this mountain village in the Cilento so that now there was music in the church.

Dottore Giuseppe di Luca, *"il Giambone"*, could play the piano beautifully –

-- operas, classics, sacral music and hymns, sometimes even more catchy, jazzy, modern tunes that had come all the way from America, which had astonished even Donato, who had not been aware of his friend's hidden talent.

The young medical man had, however, become acutely aware of Domenica, Donato's sister, and had seen her during the times at school and during his frequent visits to the D'Orsi family home.

He had watched her grow in both beauty and stature and intelligence and slowly, almost imperceptibly, he had fallen in love with her.

Propriety and professionalism had forced him to keep a respectful distance, but then, in her sixteenth year, he had, despite his great competence and rank, timorously, shyly approached her parents to ask if he could court her.

The reluctance of her parents was obvious: they told him that they were flattered for asking, but that Domenica had already been promised to young Francesco Salerno, a builder and also a mason, because their families went back so far ....

Too, although the D'Orsis would never say this publicly, this new teacher was not even really an Italian – he was a Sardo -- and had very liberal, revolutionary tendencies.

Disheartened and dispirited, he became despondent, as now his feelings of love for Domenica had become an obsession, *"un'amore folle"*, that began to affect his professional work.

There was an almost 15-year difference in their ages.

He even asked her in secret, out of a final act of desperation, to elope with him to America, but she hadn't had the courage.

The only consolation she gave him was a small picture-portrait of herself in a simple black frame.

In October 1906, *il Giambone* stands outside of the wedding ceremony of the Church, downcast, unshaven, thin, when Domenica D'Orsi is married to Francesco Salerno. Donato is the best-man.

In desperation, Dottore di Lucca returns by bicycle, by train, and steamship back to his family home in Caprera, back to his origins.

After his unexpected departure, no one talked about him any longer other than in hushed rumors that were not always positive.

Giambone never married after his heartbreaking loss in Monteforte and had kept busy with the demands of his profession, over time slowly regaining his inner composure and directed it toward helping others on his native Sardegna.

Ten years passed … until the Great War brought the old wrestling comrades together, again as conscripts of the *Granatieri di Sardegna* at the inhuman Twelfth Battle of the Isonzo: Giuseppe as the squadron's medic; Donato as one of the elite *Artigliere.*

But even a strong will and self-confidence is sometimes no match against the buffetings of fate: the final nail in Giuseppe di Lucca's dismay and disillusionment with humanity came after seeing the senseless horrors of Caporetto and the atrocities that modernity was unleashing onto simple mortals – not only advanced mechanization, but chemical agents of death.

This Great War showed the pernicious underbelly of modern progress and was nothing more than a merciless grinder of human flesh and bone.

Too, news reaches him that his beloved Mother, Beatrice, had succumbed to the ravages of *la Spagnola* while he was away tending the victims of the skirmishes, battles, fighting. His father had already passed away, many years previously.

Now, there was no one left on Sardinia for him other than some distant aged Aunts and Uncles and cousins known only by name, if even.

Although he and Donato had reinitiated their friendship, it was now more a relationship of professional respect, of familiar comrades-at-arms.

They still admired and respected one another, but as if from a far unsurmountable distance.

One year after Armistice Day, not telling any of the D'Orsis, Giuseppe di Lucca closes off the matters of his family's estate and returns to the only other place that had some meaning to him: Monteforte Cilento.

Since his departure, aging Dottore Gorga had passed away and no teacher had ever been found for any length of time or continuity.

Giuseppe saw and believed still that the innocence of youth was worth protecting and furthering despite the societal madness that continued to flare and increase around him…finally breaking out into the King's selecting a megalomaniac such as *il Duce*.

Diseases and pestilences such as polio and the Spanish flu; infestations with worms and lice and fleas; human social illnesses of the mind such as Fascism, still called up his skills now and again, but essentially, he became increasingly a shadowy recluse – appearing only now and again in the village for supplies he could not produce himself.

Too, a grandson of Dottore Gorga had followed in the elder's footsteps and was now caring for the health and well-being of his fellow townsfolk.

Sixteen years he had taught after this second return and treated maladies and breaks until he was over sixty…and then he disappeared again, once and for all now, but this time he stayed in Monteforte, somewhere in the forested flanks of Monte Chianiello.

About his presence, the townspeople were tight-lipped, especially toward the *Tedeschi* invaders that had taken strategic positions around, above, and below Monteforte Cilento.

The Giambone had watched the Germans come and go from his aerie above the village.

He knew the paths inside and out of the woods, better now even than the Montefortese themselves.

The increased bellicosity of his Italy once again disrupted any hope of continued development and education for the school children of the village.

He no longer believed too much in civilization, progress, development, let alone religion, but before falling into total despondency, he found solace in the beauty of the mountains and his crops and animals.

****

Her Mother had reached the end of her narrative and was staring off to the left, out towards and beyond the window to the unseen, ancient slopes of a mountain called Chianiello, into the darkness of the past.

Teresa Acquaviva only now realized that she was holding the embroidery needle ineffectually up in the air, unmoving, a stitch in the stylized, square-edged flower she was creating on the beige, rough-woven linen unfinished.

****

It was a cloudy, misty day in late November 1944 when the Giambone told Pasqualino Acquaviva and Giuseppe Rossi that it was time to prepare everything for the cooler, shorter days of Winter, put everything away and that they should return again on the first bright day in April after *Pasquetta* on the Second of April.

Before leaving them, he went back to a dark corner of the grotta and returned with a small object in his hand.

Looking down at the little redhead, he entrusted Giuseppe with a small wooden object, which the boy took and held delicately in his hands –

... it was two miniature figures, one of a shiny black wood, the other in a polished white wood:

-- two struggling wrestlers intertwined, but not two men; rather, they were a human and a beast – a white man and a black bear, intricately carved.

"Hide it away in your secret pocket and don't show it to anyone, Giuseppe ... I will see you at the <u>Mercato della Befana</u> and tell you what it is for."

To the older cousin, he said,

"Pasqualino, you must be the Knight, 'il Cavaliere', to protect your little cousin and this special treasure."

Then adding,

"For you, Young Man," he continued speaking to Pasqualino, *"I will have something special to ask of you at that time."*

******

Frank A. Merola

CHAPTER 19

Donato D'Orsi's carpentry shop was at the entrance to Monteforte Cilento, at the northwestern approach to the village, near a bosky area with good wood.

This proximity to the destroyed, ravaged areas, his towering stature, as well as the fine exemplars of wood-working they found when they came into his workshop, were the reasons why the Allies had called upon the still strapping 66-year-old carpenter's skills:

...the corps of engineers needed all the expert assistance they could muster to help rebuild one of the bridges on the road leading from Trentinara – the Germans had blown up at least two of them upon their planned and meticulously organized "retreat" back northward toward the Gustav line.

Their plan, their stratagem was to lure, to draw the Allies toward them to inflict as many casualties on their enemies as possible.

Coming from the direction of Trentinara, Donato's workshop was on a sloping area on the right, but the D'Orsi family had some good, wooded land also on the left side of the road and further up, amongst the ancient chestnuts in lesser accessible areas of Mount Chianiello.

Although his family had been in Monteforte for generations, the actual beginning was clouded in impenetrable mists of far chronological distances.

Perhaps they had come with the refugees from the plains below, escaping the Saracen invasions along the coast; perhaps they had come with the Normans, perhaps they had been part of an adventurous Lucanian family searching for the beneficence of salubrious mountain air.

One thing was certain, the name had to do with bears. And Donato was a tall, massive, muscular bear, and his profession helped him maintain his strength, even in his advancing years.

He had dark, curly, wiry hair, but his complexion was lighter than those in Monteforte, and he had to avoid the sun, when he could.

Although he had not shied away from the odd scuffle, invariably ending in his superiority, as a youth, wrestling, disciplined, rule-constrained wrestling, came to him only when he was on Sardinia to do his military training -- and it was there that he had first met a worthy equal: in the slightly older medical student who became his best friend, and – despite the student's smaller stature – Donato's match in the Graeco-Roman-style wrestling matches they had had.

Mens sana in corpore sano – the ancient wisdom still held true for the two young men:

Giuseppe di Lucca had been possessed and passionate about this ancient contact sport and needed it to balance out his intense studying;

Donato D'Orsi needed it, as well, to balance out his own intense, strenuous, grueling training to become a valorous and feared *"Granatiere di Sardegna"*.

As delicate, caring, and precise as the young *Dottore di Lucca* was in the medical field with injured civilians and infantrymen, and later with his suffering patients amongst the villagers, so equivalent was his unbridled, yet disciplined and bundled physical strength in the wrestling ring. No one crossed him.

Donato would never be mistaken for being delicate and caring. Precise, he was though, in the beauty and skill of his craftsmanship, of his wood- and stone-working.

Donato was the only one who could call Giuseppe di Lucca *"Giambone"* to his face … and get away with it.

******

Donato D'Orsi, as a "co-belligerent", had helped the Allies rebuild a temporary bridge – made of lumber scaffolding, essentially, but strong enough to allow tanks to cross the foresty little ravine scarring down a slope of Chianiello, on the road from Trentinara to Monteforte.

These provisional structures were named bridges "hung in the sky" and took the concerted efforts of the Americans and their local helpers only 10 hours to build.

Donato was able to help and supply beams and sinew.

His and his family's politics had always placed him on the side of "King and Country" – thus, they had supported Mussolini when *il Duce* was legitimized by Vittorio Emanuele the IIIrd, and they continued to support the King when the diminutive monarch's favor turned to Marshal Badoglio.

The preferences of the Italian regents shifted with the times and fortunes, it seemed.

Vittorio Emanuele's grandfather, Vittorio Emanuele II, had actually been the King of Sardinia and became the first King of a Unified Italy – *Padre della Patria* with the *Risorgimento*. Vittorio Emanuele the Second was a fervent supporter of the Constitution and Liberal Reforms – thus, diametrically in opposition to the politics and policies of his opportunistic grandson.

Now, Marshal General Pietro Badoglio had delegitimized the Duce, but the current King remained unscathed and simply shifted his loyalties.

Thus, Donato, too, was able to transfer his loyalties to the Allies with very little moral compunction.

For the Giambone, the acceptance of *il Duce* had been much, much more problematic; the gentle troglodyte's sentiments had always and firmly remained with the Republic, with the Constitution, with Freedom, Equality, Brotherhood, and Liberalism.

The gentry of Monteforte had been more for the old Bourbon rulers of Naples and Sicily, Royalists and pro-Church during the *Risorgimento* than the Sardinian *Repubblicani* and its centuries-long association with the House of Savoy.

Ultimately, it was these diverging political sentiments – magnified and brought to a concentrated head in this Second World War -- that had driven the "two" brothers in arms – and legs – apart.

These differences in outlook ...
... and Giuseppe's scandalous "infatuation"
with Donato's younger sister Domenica.

Frank A. Merola

Final Chapter:

At the Epiphany market, *il Mercato della Befana*, on the 6th of January 1945, as in years past, the village-folk see the reclusive Giambone coming by with his cart, pulled by his miniature black donkey, the little piebald goat on the flatbed, Mimma was not with them.

January time, cold, often misty and rainy.

People greeted him politely with *"Professó"* or *"Dottó"* and touched their hats but stared after him and whispered.

He seemed even older now, not as wound and tight with power as they had experienced him the previous year; more bent over and burdened with something invisible and dark.

There was some snow still from the previous night in the ravine on Mt. Chianiello, and a light dusting here in the village itself.

People wore their heaviest woolens.

The goats did not yet need to be taken out to their pastures, but still needed to be taken care of in their winter stalls.

Now finished with their duties to their hircine charges, Pasqualino and Giuseppe raced to the meagre, but increasingly hopeful and enthusiastic stands of the market in Monteforte's main square.

Too, the statue of San Donato had been set up in the center of the Piazza under a makeshift tarpaulin that had been given them by the American soldiers.

A massive bearded corporal had gladly helped them set it up. He must be a Catholic, the young ladies twittered hopefully amongst themselves.

Around the Saint was the warm, numinous glow of massive candles.

Struffoli, torrone, salami, freshly slaughtered pigs, and sausages redolent of fennel seeds....

What else? The boys were curious to nose around and discover!

The Giambone approached the lads from the side, silently as they were transfixed on the festival delights around them, until his presence became known to them when he asked,

"So, boys, found something you like there?"

They turned around and faced their old teacher smiling at them, delighted to see his pupils, with an almost other-worldly peace-of-mind and composure.

Giuseppe was just on the point of making a beeline to the now growing up little goat, when the Giambone gently held up a hand in a motion to stop him.

"Now, now, just wait a minute, Little One! Let me see the statue I gave you in November to guard for me, Cavaliere Giuseppe Rossi."

Now recalling his duty, Pèppe carefully, delicately took out from the hidden "war" pocket in his heavy trousers, the carved black-and-white wooden statuette of two figures frozen in the mortal embrace of a Roman wrestling battle.

He was growing up, the old man thought; the little lad had been true to his promise.

The small boy extended the statuette to his mentor, holding it reverently up in his hands.

"It is time for you to give this to my old friend Donato, my Son. He will know of its significance.

Let him know I give this to him in peace and friendship.

Put it safely away now…
… but here is something for you to keep for yourself alone."

To red-mop Pèppe he gave a wonderfully carved, beehive-shaped nuraghe, the size of a small glass jar, overturned, with a small door that, when opened, revealed a tiny shining ebony dragon.

Turning to the older cousin, *Professore* di Lucca said,

"Cavaliere Pasqualino Acquaviva, you have been true to your word and have protected the smaller, the weaker ones.

Your honor is your greatest reward, but here is something for you, for later..."

Reaching under the piebald goat, underneath its blanket, he drew out an ancient leather-bound tome of *"La Divina Commedia"*. He gave it into the lad's hands.

The odyssey of Dante and Virgil's ascent through the Underworld, Purgatory, Paradise, and their associated spiritual realms was glorified with intricate, colored lithographs of frightfully infernal and breath-takingly elysian scenes, each engraved print covered for protection in thin, delicate white transparent papers — as if clouds or eucharistic hosts had been pressed between the pages of the book like the petals of flowers....

"Soon you will be old enough to read this yourself, Pasqualino."

The two lads stood there silently, not even being able to bring a *"Grazie"* to their lips.

For Dottore Giuseppe di Lucca, their silence was more thanks than he could have expected.

Finally, as he had augured in November, the Giambone entrusted Pasqualino Acquaviva with a small dark-wooded box, instructing him to give it to his Nonna Domenica on the feast day of San Valentino.

Patting them each on the head, he thus broke the almost enraptured state the boys were in, for an enchantment had seized them that had suspended even the normal rules of propriety…the sounds of the market came back, Giambone's goat gave a complaining bleat, the world continued in its rotation.

As he had weeks before, he promised that he would see them again once the weather warmed up, on the first beautiful day after *Pasquetta*.

He would come and collect them, since he knew they would be down at their pasture.

He smiled at the boys with a twinkle squinching
his eyes, an unnoticed tear as he turned, a deep
cough heard through his short massive, now
diminishing, weakening body as he moved back up
toward the path behind the cemetery, back up to his
grotta, his books and piano, his nuraghette, his dogs
and animals.

******

The towering carpenter was surprised when the
two boys -- both were his grand-nephews --
appeared unexpectedly in his saw-and-stone-dust
filmed workshop.

They had brought him a beautiful carving, one
day after the *Mercato della Befana* – in black and white
wood – of a bear and a short powerful wiry man,
the two fighters – the beast and the man, entangled
forever in the embrace of Roman wrestlers.

Pèppe had hidden the wooden statuette in the "secret" pocket on the inside of his heavy pants – a pocket that his Nonna had sewn there into them during the war so that neither Germans nor Americans nor any other folk of ill-will would know when he was carrying anything of value ...

... like the family's golden chains and Crosses, the few lire they had, heirlooms of jewelry, sometimes even salami and eggs.

"Where did you get this, boys?"

asked Donato, turning the black-and-white object over in his immense, cut-and-calloused hands, yet with an unexpected gentleness and delicacy.

"From the Munaciedd's father."

... Giuseppe explains, but Pasqualino looks at him critically and corrects,

"Il Signore Giambone asked us to give this to you, Zio, with his greetings, and sends you wishes for peace and health in the New Year" elucidates Lino Acquaviva.

Something dark and conflicted crossed the formidable carpenter-mason's brow upon hearing the children's message, but he did not, could not, put it into words; he simply thanked them and gave them some almonds from last Autumn's harvest, but had twinges of regret…could not bring himself to forgive the troubles, fracture, disgrace, and shame the Sardinian had almost caused with his sister, nearly wreaked upon his family.

And yet….

That wily old troll, Donato thought to himself; he can even do woodworking!

He could not help but smile in wistful regret.

******

Donato *"L'Orso"* hadn't thought about his reclusive friend for a long time. This current War had consumed the day-to-day of all of them — obtaining food, protecting the women-folk, the children, their flocks and beasts, simply staying alive.

He knew the Giambone was there, up there in the mountain cave, but had kept it a secret even when the Germans had come through.

Donato respected Giuseppe di Lucca.

Yet there was both love and anger in his heart toward this man whom he had fought with – both for sport and side-by-side against a common enemy.

They had met those so many years ago when Donato had been sent by his family to join the prestigious *"Granatieri di Sardegna"*, men who loyally, valorously protected the Italian Republic with their very lives.

Familial honor was the highest principle, especially down here – even stronger than blood at times and stronger, certainly, even than the fellowship of friendship or the bonds of regimental brotherhood.

Giambone was alienated when he learned of the strength of this aspect of his comrade's character since they had both survived the macerations and inhumanity of the XIIth Battle of the Isonzo, the Battle of Caporetto where phosgene had been used.

So perfidious, so pernicious, so inhumane was that gas that it lulled one into thinking one was in a field of freshly cut hay before it ate away and corroded the skin and lungs until one died a slow death of excruciating agony through internal bleeding and final suffocation.

Their differences had nothing to do with their comradeship and loyalty on the battlefield.

Indeed, Giambone had saved Donato D'Orsi's life there near the Austrian border.

It had only been a stray, small, invisible wisp, but it had taken The Bear almost 4 months to recover; a slight asthma had remained....

No, their separation no longer had to do simply with their political differences, although these compounded the cleft.

Their ways, their beliefs had increasingly parted, their lives diverged so much so that their points of commonality had become tenuous to the point of near non-existence.

Donato had been loyal to the King even after he had sided with Mussolini and now kept his beliefs to himself…to survive the new invasion, which was gaining strength, succeeding …as it had done in the Great War.

He was left alone in his wood and stone workshop, putting the last caring touches on a simple wooden coffin for a young Texan soldier that had misstepped on a German mine, when his mind floated back to many years past on Sardinia in Sassari…

… years that were the mere blink of a stoic, distant, patient eye of the Mountain Chianiello….

The Bear thought back to Giuseppe di Lucca, then a short, strong doctor-in-training, medical student, with light brown hair and eyes of gray.

It was not easy to attribute academic prowess to him because his stature was so compact and extremely athletic in a wiry, tightly wound sort of way.

That is why Donato – *Doná* – called him
"Giambó" -- because of the power of his upper
thighs and chest and arms.

****

"Nunzio", *Annunziante*, Acquaviva, Pasqualino's
father, had been given a brief furlough, for a week,
in January but was to return North to help complete
the Liberation of Italy beyond the Gothic Line –
the defensive line Hitler had ordered his General
Kesselring rename to "The Green Line" – *Die Grüne
Linie,* for reasons of propaganda.

Annunziante Acquaviva would be needed for the
imminent Allied and partisan Spring Offensive of
1945.

The journey from the tents and temporary
encampments of Ravenna to Monteforte had been
an arduous odyssey, using any available running
trains or transports or even simple oxen-carts, but
Nunzio wanted to see his wife and child and
parents before ....

Fate had kept him safe thus far, but only the Gods knew how long this hiatus that was his life would last.

Pasqualino was overjoyed to see and sense and smell his Father once again. Giuseppe, too, not to mention Teresa....

The joy of their Father and Uncle being now with them, albeit for only a short reprieve, focused their concentration on him and their family.

The Giambone and his lessons, his recent gifts, moved unknowingly back into the shaded recesses of the grottos of their own young minds.

****

Just after mid-February of that year, the year when the war was to end, the boys learned the Giambone had died.

His remains were found on the feast day of San Valentino by Pèppe's eldest sister, Emilia.

The mature, pensive, responsible girl of sixteen-and-some had been out for a walk in the cool bright February air of the mountain, by herself, when she found a stray black donkey and heard a dog barking up in the forests, above the trickling Alento tribulet.

Despite her normal cautiousness, perhaps because of the point in her life she had reached, Emilia gathered up her courage and followed the staccato sounds and pained howlings up a path that had unexpectedly appeared, almost materialized to her upon fording the creek, and heading into, through, and up the forest.

Strange, eerie, hive-shaped structures dotted her way and seemed to bore into her back with their eye-shaped holes.

The path finally led her up to the mouth of a cave from which emanated a strange, uncommon, unpleasant odor…

The dog she found there had not been aggressive toward her, but upon seeing Emilia had ceased barking and had gone in and lay down on an old sheepskin rug by what seemed an elegantly-dressed man supine upon his bed.

Sensing immediately what the matter was, she had left the dog and the remains and gone home to tell her siblings and parents.

The fastest one, Vittorio, had gone to get his father Mauro from their masonry and metal-working shop.

****

Lino's Mamma, Zia Teresa, learned of the incident quite soon thereafter from her sister Filomena, but did not tell the youngsters immediately, nor did she recount any details.

The young mother had told Lino and Pèppe simply that *la buon'anima* Dottore di Lucca had died in peace.

Giuseppe, however, couldn't keep from inquiring of the fate of the old man's many animals.

That was the strange part, she told the lads: all the cages were empty and proper, all the mountain finches freed, the grotta swept to a guest-anticipating order and cleanliness.

Teresa's account, however, had left out an unsettling detail for she had not wanted to disturb the young boys:

... despite the truth about the cleanliness of the cave's interior and the freed finches, a rumor was circulating that perhaps something darker had happened to the occupants of the hutches just outside under the ledge near the grotta's entrance:

...the rabbits and guinea pigs had possibly escaped, but this was not certain as there were remains of desiccated, sticky bits of fur-covered pink-laced bones on the metal-mesh floors of their former homes. Nothing else....

******

Donato was with the group of men that had come together to collect the remains of Giuseppe di Lucca from his mountain cave.

Over the years of the war, the aging carpenter had become proficient at making the light, yet sturdy caskets that were a necessary accessory to life, especially in times of conflict.

For his erstwhile friend, in honor of the man's life and service, Donato had taken the time and care to brand the physician's name below a Flaming Grenade, a fireball, *il Bolide*, of their regiment's banner, onto the cover of the field coffin he had built as the doctor's final resting place.

****

Pasqualino and Giuseppe's aged mentor had been found lying in his haycot, dressed in a formal suit and tie of the late 1800's -- on his chest, underneath his interlocked, almost praying hands a paling picture of a beautiful young woman;

Beethoven's score of *"Per Elisa"* was found open on the piano.

Both objects were taken and stored away safely now by Donato, out of public sight, in a drawer in his workshop, interred amongst some of his lesser-needed carving tools -- remembrances of another time, now long past.

Too, in that very same drawer, that had become like a miniature mausoleum, there was the beautifully-crafted, pearl-studded ebony and ivory brooch, bearing the cameo image of a blindfolded Moor, facing left, on a background of gold, made by the skilled artisans of Sassari, given into his care by his little sister in a small wooden box…

…the wooden box Pasqualino had been entrusted with to give to his Nonna Domenica on the 14th of February 1945.

******

Pasqualino and Giuseppe were saddened, but their young lives went on....

They were overjoyed to receive the maturing piebald buck *Faunus*, found wandering afield of his cave by Zio Donato's own grandsons, the boys older second cousins, who had been grazing with their own herds...

... and one little dark donkey.

Tripolina was not found, but there was a dog-sized, still recent stone-covered burial mound near the edge of Giambone's glen where it began to meet the rise of the ridge, under an old fig tree.

Last and best, the boys were allowed to keep Mimma for their herd -- to Pasqualino's, but especially to Giuseppe's, delight.

Later, when they had grown up a bit more themselves, they would visit their old, beloved teacher, at least once a year on the annual feast-day of San Valentino, to pay their respects at his humble gravesite ... whose headstone was a nuraghe with the statuette of Hera in its internal alcove.

(The Goddess Hera mysteriously "disappeared" one day because Padre Massimiliano thought it was sacrilegious and idolatrous on this consecrated ground. The wily old cleric intended to have it repainted in the image of the Blessed Virgin in her cerulean blue, star-studded mantle – Hera's pomegranate could be easily enhanced into the Christ-child.

Too, he had never forgiven 'il Dottore' for one dark night furtively absconding with the church's piano he had once gifted them ... demonic forces were most certainly involved ....)

At the foot of his grave, another nuraghetta, this one with the All-Seeing Eye near its top, gazing eternally, unblinkingly toward the slope of Monte Chianiello and his former refuge.

Donato had transported these shrines from along the forest path and the cave and had placed them here.

The Giambone's dragon staff was serving as a guardian behind the entrance door of Donato D'Orsi's home.

Peace had come finally to the two wrestlers.

At the gate to the cemetery of Monteforte Cilento, these eternal Words of Warning and Wisdom:

«*Qui ha fine la superbia umana*»

An expressly inappropriate quote for him, a gifted doctor and teacher, a wrestler, a man.

Perhaps he had already done enough Purgatory?

Written on the back of his nuraghetta headstone were the simple words:

"Requiescat in Pacis"
Giuseppe di Lucca
† 14. Febbraio 1945 AD

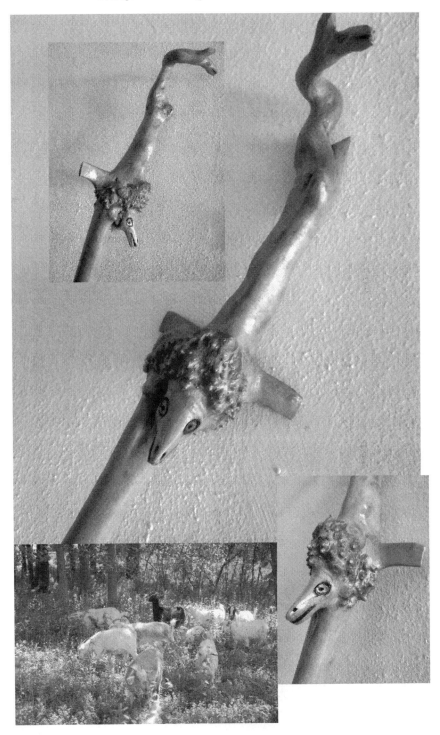

Image 1: Bombing of Monte Cassino 15. March 1944.
By IWM - http://www.iwm.org.uk/collections/item/object/205194481, Public Domain
https://commons.wikimedia.org/w/index.php?curid=33499065

Image 2: The Abbey of Monte Cassino after the February 1944 bombings.
From the Bundesarchiv, Bild 146-2005-0004 / Wittke / CC-BY-SA 3.0, CC BY-SA 3.0 de,
Public Domain https://commons.wikimedia.org/w/index.php?curid=5419752

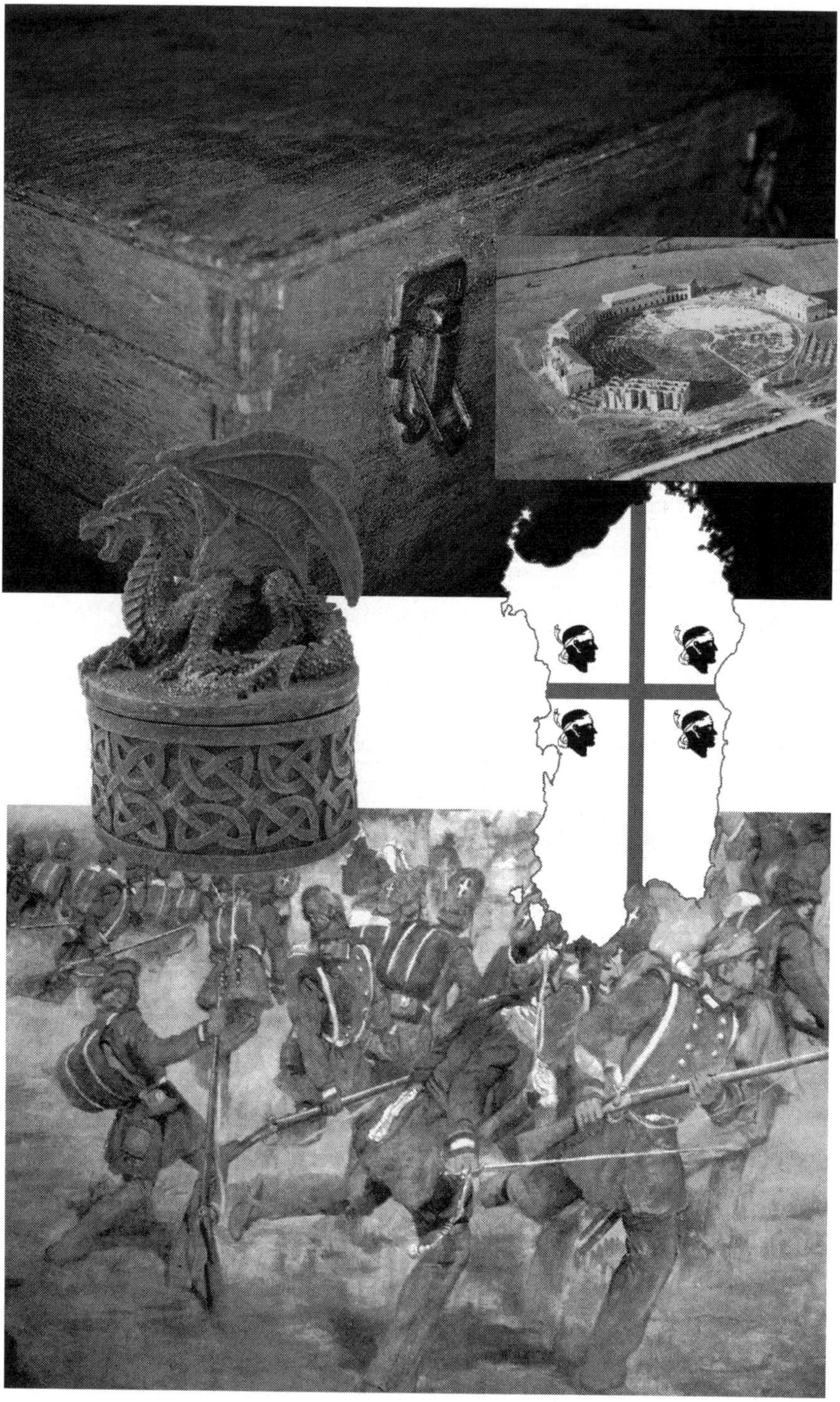

ABOUT THE AUTHOR

Frank A. (Francesco) Merola was, until his retirement in late 2017, head of a language school on Lake Zürich in Switzerland. Parallel to that he taught English and IT.

He has held management positions in various companies including ABB, World Vision, UBS, and Juventus Schools.

Writing, editing, translation, IT, family are his free-time activities. Born in Paestum (in the tobacco shop across from the temples), Campania, Salerno, Italy on August 18th, 1959, he and his family emigrated to Far Hills, New Jersey in 1962.

In 1977 he graduated from Bernards High School; in 1981 from Lehigh University. At Lehigh, he received a BSc in Psychology with minors in Biology and Italian Studies. He was inducted into Phi Beta Kappa.

In 1984 he married his Swiss wife, Beatrice, and moved to Zürich in the same year. They and their 3 children and grandchildren have been in Zürich ever since.

Frank speaks 4 languages plus 2 dialects fluently.

His other writings include:

- *Pasqualino Acquaviva and the Lupo-Mannaro*
  (In English, French, German, Italian, Campanian, Dutch, Spanish)
- *The Tower Librarian*
- *Geograffito*
- Ἐλευθερία *--Heleutheria* – under the pseudonym F. Albert Amselno
- Further adventures of Pasqualino and Giuseppe are planned….

"Can We Talk?" Press
Appenzellerstrasse 1
8049 Zürich, Switzerland
homepage.hispeed.ch/Pendragon/index.html

Ordering Information:
Quantity sales. Special discounts are available on quantity purchases by corporations, associations, educational institutions, and others.
For details, contact the publisher at the address above.
Orders by U.S. and foreign trade bookstores and wholesalers.
Please contact "Can We Talk?" Press Distribution:
Tel: (+41) 078 606-2609;
Fax: n.a.;
E-mail: pendragon@swissonline.ch

Printed in Switzerland, Italy, Germany, The Netherlands, and the United States of America

Publisher's Cataloging-in-Publication data
Merola, Frank Albert
"Pasqualino Acquaviva and Giambone" / Frank A. Merola
p. 6 cm. *
ISBN 978-1-98308-520-8
1. The main category of the book — Cultural heritage: Southern Italian, Campania
2. Historical Fiction
3. Family Life
I. Frank Albert Merola.
II. "Pasqualino Acquaviva and Giambone"
HF0000.A0 A00 2010
299.000 00–dc22 2010999999

First Edition (*primum emendatione*)

14 13 12 11 10 / 10 9 8 7 6 5 4 3 2 1